A DC KENDRA MARCH CRIME THRILLER

BORN TO KILL

Book 7 of the 'Summary Justice' series

Theo Harris

Copyright © 2024 by Theo Harris
All rights reserved.

Paperback ISBN: 979-8-324079-57-4

No part of this book may be reproduced in any form or by any electronic or
mechanical means, including information storage and retrieval systems,
without written permission from the author, except for the use of brief
quotations in a book review.

This is a work of fiction. Names, characters, places, and incidents are either
the product of the author's imagination or are used fictitiously, and any
resemblance to actual persons, living or dead, business establishments,
places of learning, events or locales is entirely coincidental.

PRAISE FOR THEO HARRIS

'Couldn't put the book down. Loved it.'

'The pacing of the book was impeccable, with each chapter leaving me hungry for more.'

'WOW! I was not expecting much but totally surprised.'

'One of my favourite reads of the year, waiting for the rest of the series!'

'Really gripping storytelling that is clearly well researched and engaging.'

Cool gritty romp... Excellent lead character and plot - really enjoyed the story.'

**Before AN EYE FROM AN EYE...
There was**

TRIAL RUN

An exclusive Prequel to the **'Summary Justice'** series, free to anyone who subscribes to the Theo Harris monthly newsletter.

Find out what brought the team together and the reasons behind what they do... and why.

Go to **theoharris.co.uk**
or join at:
https://dl.bookfunnel.com/7oh5ceuxyw

ALEMAR
PUBLICATIONS

ALSO BY THEO HARRIS

Also by Theo Harris

DC Kendra March - 'Summary Justice' series

Book 1 - An Eye for an Eye

Book 2 - Fagin's Folly

Book 3 - Road Trip

Book 4 - London's Burning

Book 5 - Nothing to Lose

Book 6 - Justice

Book 7 - Born to Kill

Boxset 1 - Books 1 to 3

Boxset 2 - Books 4 to 6

Boxset 3 - Books 1 to 6

Think you've gotten away with it? Think again!

PROLOGUE

As the crowds grew in number they also grew in confidence. They surged through the streets of central London, chanting mottos directed at the government's failures, foreign policies, religions other than their own, and just about everything they demanded be fixed to appease them. They even demanded that certain comedians be beheaded for telling jokes that didn't sit well with their own moral compasses.

By late afternoon, there were tens of thousands of them, from all over the country, from various disgruntled communities, all wanting to voice their concerns, all angry with a government they believed was failing them, and, for some, insulting them and their beliefs. Stealthily, a sinister little group wormed its way through the crowd, looking for those with prominent voices, those they could agitate into doing more than just shouting and screaming at the unseen enemy. They had a plan, and this was the perfect place—and the perfect time—to carry it out.

At dusk, the agitators started directing and cajoling their

new-found friends, pointing at buildings of supposed enemies, at expensive, flash cars that were parked close by. At first, they threw the odd tin can or plastic bottle, denting parked cars and staining shop windows with fruit juice. The accompanying police escort did nothing, other than keeping them within the metal barricades that had been erected in anticipation of the demonstration. One of the agitators then picked up one of the barriers, disconnecting it easily from the others and throwing it at one of the shop windows, cracking the heavy, expensive pane of glass. This elicited a roar of approval from the crowd, which was gaining in conviction and getting angrier by the minute.

The police started to take notice, especially as they were now forced to acknowledge they were severely outnumbered. They hadn't been expecting any serious violence, and were certainly ill-prepared for it. Still, they did nothing, electing to wait in the hope that it was a one-off; that it was little more than a peaceful demonstration, as the organisers had so vehemently claimed. They were wrong... badly wrong. Within just a couple of minutes, the crowd surged to the sides and started taking the barriers apart, throwing them at shops, at the defenceless police escort, and at parked vehicles. Within ten minutes, cars were on fire and the area was deemed an exclusion zone, with riot police called in to deal with the escalating violence.

Thirteen officers were badly hurt before the riot officers and dog handlers arrived. Mounted police joined them soon after, charging at the crowd to disperse them, whilst guiding them to the smaller side streets where they could be more easily contained, and where units from the riot squads were waiting. The violence lasted just forty minutes, but the lasting damage to both property and persons was done, including one department store looted and set on fire in its entirety; violent enough to feature on news channels both domestic and foreign. Seventeen demonstrators were arrested, including several who had been influenced by the agitators.

That small, sinister group of agitators, who had played such a significant part in the violence, split up, got rid of clothing that could identify them, and made their separate ways back to East London, where they laughed and congratulated each other. It had been so very easy.

'Tomorrow, you know what to do. Do it in the open and in front of witnesses, and remember to shout the words you've been practising,' said their enigmatic leader as he nodded gratefully to his subordinates.

Loud cheers followed before he quietened them with his hand gestures.

'After tomorrow, nobody will think of crossing us again. Ever.'

1

THE CUBE

'I have to say, they've done a grand job,' Andy said, as he admired the new building that stood proudly behind the factory, its newly fabricated panels gleaming in the sun.

The 'factory,' which was the name the team had bestowed upon their headquarters, had been bought with Albanian gang money and was situated on a large plot near Tilbury Docks, by the river Thames. The team headquarters housed a legitimate security business, *Sherwood Solutions*, where members of the team, particularly the younger ones, had learned their trades and helped build what was becoming a successful business. To that end, the front of the building was professionally laid out, with reception staff to greet visitors and guide them to meeting rooms to discuss security solutions and products.

The back end of the factory was a different animal altogether. That was where the reinforced rooms were, temporary holding cells to house the criminal 'guests' until they were moved elsewhere, sometimes thousands of miles away...

or *disposed of*, for want of a better term. Disposed of, like the trash they were.

There were also training rooms, and others to store the equipment the team had acquired over the past couple of years, some of it illegal and some of it borderline.

Their cause was simple: dispense justice to criminals who would otherwise get away with their crimes, as the law was ineffective or out of date, and the police were effectively handcuffed, hamstrung, and frustrated by their diluted powers, a legacy of poor government decisions going back decades. The team had done so, effectively, ridding the streets of London of some very nasty individuals, with a by-product bonus of 'acquiring' their wealth, which would later fund their venture, somewhat illegal but hugely effective and satisfying morally... and ironic, to boot. There were many occasions where the team laughed at the irony of the criminals funding their own downfalls.

The resulting success and fortune had led to the team building the new structure behind the factory. It now housed a state-of-the-art ground-floor showroom for the modern security equipment and professional security services, including research and development, run by Charmaine. Upstairs, an equally impressive training centre was run by Amir, who had come up with the idea of the one-stop shop.

The building had taken only a few months, thanks mainly to the prefabricated framework and outer shell. Then came the internal insulation, fittings, and decorating, before the equipment was brought in to complete the two-storey project.

'It's a good job you're a bit of an expert at stealing money from the criminals, otherwise none of this would be possible,' Trevor said, referring to Andy's outstanding hacking abilities.

'Yeah, good job, handsome,' Kendra added, winking at a blushing Andy.

'Well, now that it's done, it'll be interesting to see how Charmaine and Amir get on with it, seeing as you've given them free rein,' Andy said.

'They'll be fine, and if you recall, I asked Mo to oversee the whole thing, just in case.' Trevor smiled.

'Are we gonna give it a name? We can't call them both *the factory*, can we?' asked Kendra.

'How about *the Thunderdome*, like in Mad Max?' said Andy.

Trevor and Kendra looked at him quizzically.

'I guess that's a no, then?'

'You guessed correctly,' Trevor said

'Why *did* we name the factory the way we did?' Kendra mused.

'Because that's where all the work was happening?' Andy replied.

'That's about right, it was an easy one to name. Why don't we apply the same logic to name this shiny new building?' she said.

'Well, there's gonna be some training upstairs and a flash showroom downstairs, it won't be as easy, methinks,' Trevor added, scratching the back of his head.

'The gym? The office?' Andy said out loud, hoping something would stick.

'Yeah, I don't think either of those work in this case, it's two different scenarios,' Trevor said.

'Let's just keep it simple, then,' Kendra said, 'if we can't go with something that describes the goings-on, then we just use something to describe the exterior.'

'The tin can?' Andy laughed.

'The cube,' Kendra said. 'It pretty much is that shape, so why not?'

Trevor nodded. 'Works for me!'

'You'll get no argument from me,' Andy said, 'that's pretty accurate and rolls off the tongue.'

'It's settled, then, the cube it is. Let's go and get ready to officially open it to the team and our future guests,' Trevor said.

'I'm excited about that,' Kendra said, 'if you can get some of your old forces friends to take an interest, we can get some very nice contracts out of it.'

'I'm sure we can,' Trevor said, 'but let's not lose sight of what we're doing behind the scenes, eh? The legitimate business will allow us to hire more people and get a few more youngsters off the street, and that for me is a priority.'

'Amen to that,' Andy said, 'but getting rid of criminals should always remain our prime objective.'

'And it will be, don't you worry,' Kendra said.

'So, how many people are coming tonight?' Andy asked, referring to the small gathering they'd invited for some canapes and soft drinks.

'With the team, I think there'll be around thirty to forty in total, it should be interesting,' said Trevor.

'We've briefed the team, to make sure they don't say too much to the guests. Other than those who already know, we don't want anyone to learn what we do behind the scenes, okay?' Trevor said.

'Agreed,' said Kendra. Andy nodded.

'I'll go and get everyone.' Trevor made his way back to the factory.

'Let's go and get ready to greet them, handsome,' Kendra said, turning and walking towards the cube.

'Such a tease,' Andy muttered, following.

'WELCOME, everyone, to Sherwood Solution's new state-of-the-art showroom and training centre,' Trevor said to the group of people gathered in the ground-floor showroom. 'As you can see, we have some new equipment already installed, but you can be assured there will be much more to follow.'

There was a smattering of applause and some *whoops*, mainly from the team members who had mingled with the guests.

'We're affectionately calling it *the cube*, so if you hear that term from now on, you know what it refers to,' Kendra said.

'As you can see,' added Trevor, 'we've laid out some drinks and a nice selection of hors d'oeuvres by the side there, please help yourselves. Take all the time you need to look around, both downstairs and up, and if you have any questions, you can ask me or Kendra, but also Charmaine or Amir, who will be running the showroom and training centre respectively.'

The guests made their way to the refreshments as Trevor and Kendra shook hands with them. Kendra could see Andy at the back, standing with Detective Sergeant Rick Watts, her boss at the Special Crimes Unit, where she worked part-time. He was now fully engaged with the team, which enhanced their ability to gather intelligence that only police officers had access to.

'Nicely said, Dad. You seem to have the knack of public speaking, it suits you,' Kendra teased, linking her proud father's arm.

'When you've given as many briefings as I have, you get used to it,' he said, referring to his secretive past as an undercover officer in the British Army.

'So, tell me again who you invited.'

'One of the first people I contacted was the First Sea Lord and Chief of Naval Staff, Admiral Sir Robert Jenkins, mainly because of his assistance in taking down the Triads last year.'

'He's the one whose life you saved about a hundred years ago, isn't he?' She laughed.

'It wasn't quite a hundred years, love, but it was a few decades ago when he was just a regular navy officer posted to Northern Ireland. Anyway, he's here with a couple of other bigwigs to see what we're offering as a security company.'

'What do you think they'd be interested in?'

'I'm hoping we can apply for the contract for the base security, you know, guarding the perimeter, CCTV, access control, that sort of thing.'

'Are we set up to do that?' Kendra asked, recognising that Sherwood Solutions had been a registered company for only a couple of years.

'It won't be easy, but I have a plan to recruit ex-staff who are looking for jobs, and I have a friend who runs a recruitment company along those lines. Unless you have a go, you won't know, will you?'

'Fair enough. Who else did you invite?'

'Mike Romain, an ex-colleague of mine, who joined around the same time as me. He ended up as a colonel in army intelligence, so I worked with him a few times. He's retired now, but runs a surveillance company. He recently obtained a contract to investigate a number of very large sports organisations for corruption. He'll be looking for surveillance equipment and possibly personnel, and he's here with a couple of other directors from his company.'

'Sounds very promising. Even one of those contracts would be a huge boost,' Kendra said.

'I'm pretty confident; knowing who to call is a big part of getting things done, isn't it? I'm not counting my chickens just yet, but we have more than enough on offer to interest any company.'

'I agree. Getting the cube built was a great idea and shows we mean business. I have to say, Charmaine and Amir showed a different side of themselves, didn't they? The way they've conducted themselves through the build has been fantastic, and in Amir's case, surprisingly professional,' Kendra said.

Trevor laughed.

'Yeah, he can be a clown, but underneath it all he is a very shrewd young man.'

'Let's mingle, then, Dad. You can introduce me to some of these bigwig friends of yours,' she said, grabbing his arm again.

'FIVE-FIVE-SEVEN, ARE YOU RECEIVING, OVER?' the message sounded over the radio.

'Received loud and clear, November whisky, five-five-seven, over,' replied police constable Ray Khan.

'We've just had a call from the Menorah Jewish school in The Drive, they've had someone call with death threats. Can you deal?'

'All received, November whisky, show me as dealing. Five-five-seven, over,' Ray replied.

He wasn't surprised to hear threats had been made, considering the problems the day before, and in the past, where Jewish establishments had been targeted. Knowing the levels of security in place gave Ray confidence that the risk was low, providing everyone at the school remained vigilant. It was his job as the local community officer to attend and reassure them.

He parked the marked police car in Woodstock Avenue, where there were plenty of spaces. Exiting the car, he put on his favoured flat cap, locked the car, and walked towards the school entrance, clipboard in hand.

Ray didn't take any notice of the silver BMW saloon parked a few cars behind his, nor did he see the two men exit that car and walk towards him with purpose, as he made his way to the junction. He did see a woman pushing a pram put her hand to her mouth as she watched him, and wondered what that was about. It was when she screamed that he realised something was wrong, and turned back to see what had frightened her so much.

For Ray, it all happened in slow motion. Two men in dark clothing, each brandishing a black handgun, were almost upon him. He saw the flashes and heard the awful, astonishingly loud gunshots at the same time as the two bullets struck him: one in the chest and one in the stomach. The last thing he heard was his killers shouting.

'Allahu Akbar! Allahu Akbar! Allahu Akbar!'

He didn't have time to think or to ask the question – 'Why?'

His vision went black, and he was dead before he hit the

ground, the clipboard still in his hand and his flat cap now lying next to his lifeless body.

The woman with the pram continued to scream, and she was joined by two other passers-by who had witnessed the brutal assassination in broad daylight.

The killers were back in their car and away before anyone could react. The registration number of the car was noted by one of the witnesses, and although the vehicle was found abandoned and on fire later that evening, there would be no incriminating evidence to indicate who had been responsible.

The only clue was what the witnesses had heard, the killers' chant.

THE EVENING WAS ALMOST OVER, and most guests had gone when a middle-aged, grey-haired man approached Trevor and Kendra. He was smartly dressed in a navy-blue suit, crisp white shirt and no tie, and black shoes. Flanked by two slightly younger men, also well-dressed, the man extended his hand, which Trevor grasped warmly before bringing him in for a bear hug.

'I thought you were ignoring me, you old goat!' Trevor grinned. 'You've just turned up for the free grub, haven't you? Not to see your old mate.'

'Well, if you put it like that... maybe it was to check out your flash products and services, eh?' the man said, before turning to Kendra and taking her hand. 'You must be the delightful daughter this guy won't stop talking about. I'm Mike... Mike Romain.'

Kendra shook his hand warmly.

'I'm sorry about the stories, it's only recently that I've realised Dad talks a lot more than I ever thought,' she said, turning to Trevor and grinning.

'Yeah, well, spare a thought for me. I had to listen to him talking non-stop for years!' Mike laughed.

'You worked together in the army?'

'You could call it that, yes. We were in army intelligence together for a few years, mainly in Northern Ireland and a couple of other hot spots. All joking aside, he may have talked a lot, but he was bloody good at his job, we missed him badly when he upped and left.'

'I had to leave, Mike, it was all getting a bit boring, wasn't it? You lot didn't want us to have fun anymore.'

'You should have seen just how boring it was when I got promoted, mate. I spent years regretting it and missing that fun that you mentioned,' Mike said, recalling their adventures. 'Where are my manners? These two fine gentlemen are my fellow directors, Brandon Finch and Haydn Brown. Gents, this is my old mucker from the army that I told you about, the slippery one.'

They all laughed and exchanged handshakes.

'Thank you for such an inspiring introduction, Mike. Moving on quickly, we're glad you're here today, we've been excited to get the place open so we can show you what we can do. Seen anything that appeals to you?' Trevor asked.

'Some things, yes,' Brandon said, 'there was some nice surveillance kit that your geek was showing us earlier, especially the miniature stuff. Where do you source it all?'

'You know that geek you mentioned? He can sniff that stuff out before it's even released. He's very well-connected and knowledgeable so it gives us a nice edge over the competition, which as a new company we need,' Kendra said.

'It was impressive,' Mike said. 'I think we can work together on a couple of projects for sure, Trevor. How are you fixed for operatives? We're always looking for talented people who can mingle unnoticed.'

'Without boasting too much, we have a fine young team that can get into any place without attracting attention. They've honed those skills over the last couple of years and we've had some excellent results. What are you thinking?' Trevor asked, concerned that he may lose some of his team.

'Don't worry, I promise I won't poach your people. I'm thinking more that we can hire your team when we're short, that sort of thing.'

'Or vice versa?'

'Absolutely, scratching each other's backs is a no-brainer, don't you think?' Mike said.

'Let's talk again soon, Mike, it seems we have a few options worthy of a chat,' said Trevor.

'Definitely, Trev. It was great seeing you again, buddy.' Mike gave Trevor a parting hug. 'Good to meet you also, Kendra, finally!'

Mike and his team departed, leaving Trevor and Kendra to look around. There were a few of the team still loitering, talking in small groups or cleaning up.

'I'd say that was a big success, wouldn't you, Dad?'

'It's not over yet, sweetheart, I have someone waiting to speak with us privately. Sir Robert is waiting for us in the meeting room over at the factory, he wants to discuss a huge business opportunity.'

'It's good to see you again, Trevor. Nice set-up you have here,' Sir Robert said, shaking Trevor's hand. 'This is Captain Richard Tremayne and Commander Valerie Upton, who are here on behalf of the Admiralty procurement department. I persuaded them, gently, that it would be a good idea to come and speak with you.'

'That's very kind, thank you, sir. Welcome, to you both,' Trevor said. 'This is my daughter, Kendra, a serving police detective with the Met.'

'It's good to meet you all,' she said.

'I'm guessing you're here about the perimeter security at bases. Unfortunately, we don't have all the equipment installed yet, but you'll be very pleased with what we'll be able to offer,' Trevor said. 'In terms of staff, that depends on your requirements, but I have every confidence that we can fulfil them.'

'Actually, that's not why we're here, Trevor. Yes, there is a contract coming up for the bases, but we're more interested in speaking with you regarding some... how do you say... unofficial arrangements?' the First Sea Lord replied.

'Um, not sure what to say here. What do you mean by unofficial arrangements?' Trevor asked, caught somewhat by surprise.

'It's a rather delicate matter that we should sit down and discuss in private,' Sir Robert replied. 'Is there somewhere we can sit and talk?'

'We have a canteen upstairs,' Kendra said, beckoning them towards the stairs.

They made their way to the first floor, after she had spoken briefly with Charmaine to explain they'd be in a private meeting, and to ask if she could take over downstairs and see everyone off. Trevor made some hot drinks, and soon, they were all seated around the table waiting on Sir Robert to explain.

'About four months ago, we heard rumours that someone was stealing weapons from a navy base somewhere in the south and selling them to drug gangs in London. We did some inventory checks and found everything to be in order, nothing missing, and dismissed the rumours out of hand. About a month later, we were contacted by a detective from Brixton, in south London, about an SA80 A2 self-loading rifle that had been seized during a house search for a multiple murder suspect, who had shot and killed two people in a drive-by shooting. The detective told us that the serial number had been scratched off but recovered by forensics, and it was one of ours. It was the weapon used to kill those people. This led to a second, more thorough inventory check, which resulted in a disturbing discovery,' Sir Robert said.

'I'm afraid to ask,' Trevor replied.

'It's actually a lot worse than you might think. When we opened the boxes at Stonehouse Barracks, we found that the new SA80s had somehow been replaced with old stock, and the boxes resealed to make it seem nothing was amiss.'

'What? How was that possible?' Trevor asked.

'There's more. It turns out that the old stock was actually weaponry that had been handed in during a firearms amnesty in London recently and which had been earmarked for destruction.'

'Wait, you're saying that someone stole weapons from the Met and then stole newer weapons from Three Brigade Commando and replaced them with the old crap without anyone knowing?' Kendra said.

'That's the sum of it, yes.'

'Do you have any suspects?' asked Trevor.

'Only one, colour sergeant Reg Malone, the armourer at the time we believe the switch was made.'

'Is he in custody?' Kendra asked.

'Nope. He went AWOL and hasn't been seen since.'

'Bloody hell, that's a hell of a scenario, sir,' Trevor said, shaking his head in disbelief.

'How many weapons were taken, Sir Robert?' Kendra asked.

'One hundred SA80s.'

'Wow, that's a lot of serious weaponry,' she said, 'got any ideas as to whether they are all on the streets now?'

'I don't think so, hence my coming here. We think a handful were sold and the rest are being stored somewhere in London, but we've come up short. Think your team can help us?' Sir Robert asked, smiling at his old friend.

'We can certainly try,' Trevor said, 'as long as you're okay with us using unofficial methods.'

'Oh, don't worry about that, this operation will be entirely off the books, and you'll be paid by a shell company that can't be traced back to us,' Sir Robert said, winking.

'We'll be paid for it too, eh? That's a nice, unexpected result, I guess it was worth sending you that invite!' Trevor laughed.

'Don't think I've forgotten about the upcoming security contract, either. If you can prove you can do a good job for us, then there's a good chance that will come your way also. Commander Upton will send you the official documentation for that.'

'I'll just need your contact details, sir, and I can get that to you tomorrow, first thing,' Upton said.

'Can you give us all the information you have to hand about the guns?' Kendra asked.

'Of course, Captain Tremayne will liaise with you and stay in touch moving forward, I hope that doesn't cause any issues. I don't want him treading on your toes.'

'I'm sure we can manage. Here's my card, please send everything and I'll update you regularly with any progress,' Kendra said, handing Tremayne her Sherwood Solutions business card.

'Yes, ma'am, I look forward to working with you,' Tremayne replied.

The visitors left soon after, leaving Trevor and Kendra alone in the deserted showroom.

'That took a weird turn, didn't it?' she said.

'It certainly did, a very *interesting* turn, too,' Trevor replied.

2

REVELATIONS

Trevor, Andy and Kendra arrived at the factory early the following morning, expecting a flurry of emails and information relating to the theft and also the forthcoming contract tender.

'And he actually said we'll be paid for doing this?' Andy asked, surprised and pleased at the same time.

'That he did, yes,' Trevor replied, 'which is a very good thing, because if we can prove ourselves with this job then there's every chance we'll be in pole position for the security contract.'

'Along with any other *unofficial* work they're very likely to have,' Kendra added, 'which could be very lucrative to our growing business.'

'Wow, so building the cube may have already paid for itself with just one evening's worth of schmoozing. Nice!' Andy said.

'The email about the forthcoming contract is here; has Upton sent anything about the guns, yet, love?'

'No, but it's still early, I'm sure it'll be here soon,' Kendra replied.

'I'll have a look through this security contract while you're waiting,' Trevor said. 'Andy, any chance you can do a little digging on the dark web about the availability of some shiny new rifles?'

'I can make a start, for sure. There's a couple of shifty dealers on there who I bought some kit from last year, I'm sure if anyone knows, they will.'

'I'll go and check the cube to see if anything needs tidying up while I wait for Tremayne to come through,' Kendra said, walking off.

Within an hour, most of the rest of the team arrived, the majority of them working on Sherwood Solutions business and a few helping Charmaine and Amir to familiarise themselves with their respective departments in the new building.

It was late morning when a courier arrived with a parcel addressed to Kendra.

'You have to hand it to them, they're not taking many chances with anything being traced to them,' she told Trevor and Andy, when they had reconvened. 'Everything they know is right here in this folder, with all traces of the military removed.'

'If you're going to do something then do it right, or so the experts say,' Andy replied, nodding appreciatively.

'It looks like a hefty bundle of papers there, love. Does it look like it's anything useful for us?'

'Yeah, it's pretty thorough, to be honest. All the serial numbers, the specs, times, dates, suspect information, there's a lot for us to start with, including some info about the Brixton shootings, which I can follow up on at work tomorrow.'

'Okay, you can take charge of all that, with Andy's help, of course. I'll focus on this for now, there's not a lot else going on,' Trevor said, just as Mo and Amir appeared, along with their mother, Jasmine. Their expressions suggested something was very wrong.

'That may be about to change, boss,' Amir said.

'Hello, Jasmine, it's great to see you. Is everything alright?' Trevor asked, helping her to a chair.

'Hello, Trevor, I am sorry to trouble you, but I couldn't think of anyone else who could help. The twins said it would be okay to speak with you, I hope they weren't out of turn.'

'Not at all, they're absolutely right to do so. Tell me, what's the problem?'

'A friend of mine came to see me yesterday. He was in a terrible state, crying and howling, like he was in great pain. When he eventually calmed down, he told me that his son had been killed as punishment because of a debt that he had, the father. The murderers are now threatening to kill the rest of his family unless he gives them the hotel that he owns. Please, can you help him?' Jasmine pleaded.

'They killed his son because he owed money?' Kendra said, 'that sounds extreme, how much money was involved?'

'It was two hundred and fifty thousand pounds, he borrowed it during the pandemic when he lost a lot of business, so that he could pay for taxes and renovations. Because it went on for so long, he's not had a chance to pay the money back yet, and now they have killed his son. His son was a wonderful young man, his family were so proud when he became a police officer.'

'Wait, what?' Kendra exclaimed, 'are you talking about Ray Khan, who was shot yesterday?'

'Yes, do you know him?'

'Not personally, but when a colleague is killed in the Met, we all get to know about it very quickly. There's a massive hunt for the killers now, early indications are that he was targeted by terrorists,' Kendra said.

'Miss Kendra, I don't think it was terrorists, the people my friend had dealings with were from Vietnam, they are loan sharks.'

'Really? From what I've heard on the grapevine, the investigators are convinced it was a terrorist attack on a Jewish school that went wrong; that the PC was just in the wrong place at the wrong time,' Kendra replied.

Jasmine shook her head.

'No, no, my friend is convinced it is the loan sharks, they are very bad people and they have been taking over businesses all over the place by hurting people—and worse. He told me that a few have disappeared completely, nobody knows whether they have run away, or if they are buried somewhere,' Jasmine insisted.

'Well, I guess this contract can wait, this is something we need to look into. Where is your friend now, Jasmine?' Trevor said.

'He's at the hotel, trying to put his affairs in order. I think he is going to give them the hotel to stop anybody else from dying. He is desperate, Mr Trevor.'

'Do you think he will talk to us?' Kendra asked.

'Yes, I am sure he would, but please do it carefully, he doesn't want the police involved any more than they have to be,' Jasmine replied.

'Please call him and ask if we can go and speak to him,' Trevor said. 'I want to know as much about these people as possible before we decide what to do.'

As Trevor and Kendra approached the hotel, they saw that it was in a prime location close to good transport links that included City Airport, modern shopping facilities at Canary Wharf, and an expanding industrial park. Jasmine had told them that Kamal Khan, her friend, had purchased the hotel soon after it was built during the London Docklands regeneration of the nineties. The hotel had thrived for the next twenty years or so and it was only in the past five years that it had started to struggle, primarily due to the more modern and luxurious competition that had been built. Kamal Khan had borrowed heavily to renovate the hotel in an attempt to bring back some of the earlier success. The attempt hadn't been immediately successful, but Kamal was confident and had plans in place to change that within two years. The banks, however, did not share his confidence and demanded repayment of the loans with short notice, suggesting he sell the hotel to repay his debts.

The hotel owner resisted the bank's advice to sell and went to see a friendly, local businessman he knew. Unbeknownst to Kamal, the businessman had recently affiliated himself with a powerful new entity in the area, loan sharks of a different ilk. He received his commission for the introduction and walked away from his friend, leaving Kamal at the mercy of the loan sharks. Despite this, he was confident his plan would work, as the agreements he had in place were due to take effect. And then COVID had struck and his plans had rapidly disintegrated, leaving him bereft and at the mercy of the Vietnamese gang. He pleaded for more time, which was not given. He failed to pay back an instalment that was due, and had had an arm broken as a result.

'That was your one and only warning,' the loan shark had told him as he lay on the ground in agony. 'Next time, we will bring death to your door.'

They were true to their word, and now Kamal's only son was dead.

When Trevor and Kendra walked into the hotel there was nobody at reception and no guests in sight. It was eerily quiet.

'This isn't what you'd expect when going into a hotel, is it?' Kendra said, looking around in confusion.

'Maybe he closed after the shooting,' Trevor replied.

'Let's stay here, we're being watched,' she said, pointing to the CCTV camera that was focused on them, its red light blinking. She waved at it.

A minute later, a man stepped into reception from a nearby doorway. In his mid-to-late fifties, he looked dishevelled in a grey suit and blue shirt, his eyes still wet from crying.

'Are you Jasmine's friends?' he asked, looking around fearfully.

'Yes, Mr Khan, we'd like to talk to you about your son's murder,' Kendra said, 'and to try and help you with your problems.'

'It's too late, I can't risk them killing anyone else, they can have the hotel, to hell with them all,' Khan replied angrily.

'Mr Khan, we can protect you and your family if you'd let us, we know your predicament is serious, but we have experience in dealing with people like the ones who killed your son. Please, just spare us some of your time and we can explain,' Trevor said.

Khan eventually relented, and beckoned them to the door he had come through. It led to a corridor with offices on one side, all empty of staff, until they came to a door at the end.

'This is my office, we can talk in here,' Khan said, letting them in.

The office was spacious and elegantly furnished with Indian furniture and art, with an L-shaped leather settee at one end and an antique mahogany desk at the other.

'Please, sit.'

'Mr Khan, can you tell me how much you still owe these people?' Kendra asked.

'It's about two hundred and fifty thousand pounds,' he said, looking at the floor as if embarrassed.

'What did you borrow the money for?'

'Along with an overdue tax bill, we used the money to renovate the rooms and bring everything up to a more luxurious standard. The project actually cost close to a million pounds; we used all our savings, but needed the rest to finish the project. COVID hit us very badly, we'd signed an agreement with a large oversees hotel chain for their London business, which was worth millions to us, and which would have paid everything we owe, quickly. If it was anyone other than a bloody loan shark, we would have recovered quickly, but they want the hotel and they know how valuable it is here. I've already lost my son, and now I will lose everything else,' he said, burying his head in his hands and weeping.

'Mr Khan, I'm sorry for your loss, but please don't give in, these bastards can be beaten and we can help you, I promise.'

He looked up at his guests and shook his head.

'They are too powerful. They're using local gangs to do their dirty work, they've been coming round scaring our customers away and smashing the windows of local businesses. There's too many of them.'

'We'll need you to tell us all about them, as much as you can, but before we do that, can you tell us where your family are?' Trevor asked.

'My wife and daughter are upstairs, out of the way. We daren't go back to our house,' Khan said, 'they know where we live so I brought them here as it will be harder to find them.'

'I want you to call them and pack what you can, okay? We're going to take you somewhere safe, somewhere far from here. We'll take care of your hotel and your home until you're ready to come back. Can you do that?' Trevor asked.

Khan nodded.

'I will go and get them now, we are already packed and ready,' he said, 'give me a few minutes.'

'We'll get someone to pick you up and take you to safety, and someone to stay here at the hotel. Do you have any guests here?'

'No, the last of them left this morning, we had to cancel all bookings and ask people to leave early, after what happened.'

'We'll need the keys to the hotel and your home. Leave the rest to us,' Trevor said.

Khan nodded and made his way from the office to collect his family.

'I'll call Darren and have him bring a car to pick them up. Who do you have in mind to look after the hotel?' Kendra asked.

'Let's get the twins here with Charmaine, Zoe, and a couple of Darren's boys. Six of them should be able to hold the fort until we can reinforce our position here,' said Trevor.

Kendra called the team and made the request.

'Darren is sending Jimmy and Izzy to pick the family up. Where do you want to take them?'

Trevor grinned.

'I have just the place, but the owner may not like it!'

'Are you for real?' Brodie Dabbs asked, not knowing whether to believe what Trevor had requested. 'I've just got this place finished exactly how I wanted it and you're asking me to take in a bunch of strangers?'

'I know it's short notice, but they're in real danger and I couldn't think of a safer place to send them than your lovely farm,' Trevor said, referring to the newly renovated farmhouse that former gang leader Dabbs had moved into in his semi-retirement. He wanted to be away from London but with his fingers in a few lucrative pies to keep him interested, and the farmhouse was the perfect bolthole, far from all the problems associated with his former gang-related business interests.

'You know my missus is gonna throw a fit, don't you? She's been spending my money like nobody's business getting the place kitted out exactly how she wants it, and now I have to tell her we have people coming? Christ, Trev, you know how to ruin our week, don't you?'

'It shouldn't be for too long, and you can put them in the granny annex, can't you? They won't be in your way at all, I'm sure.'

'That place is for her mum, who's due here next week. I built that place especially to keep her out of our bloody house, and now because of you she'll have to stay with us, right next door to our bloody bedroom,' Brodie grunted.

Trevor tried hard not to laugh, coughing to cover his mirth.

'Look, I'll make it up to you, okay? These loan sharks have got something big going on here, it might be something you can get involved in when we've done our thing,' he said.

He knew that he had Brodie hooked when his friend paused.

'You'd better be right, Giddings, or I'll have the right hump with you,' Brodie said. 'I expect regular updates, and at some point, you can tell me what it'll be worth to me.'

'Great, my boys will be there with the family in a couple of hours, okay? Thanks again, Brodie,' Trevor said, hanging up before Brodie could change his mind.

'You enjoyed that, didn't you?' Kendra said as her dad wiped away a tear.

'Yeah, that was fun. I'll make it up to him, don't worry. Let's go and make a coffee while we plan what we're going to do next.'

3

COMING UP SHORT

Kendra and Trevor met with Andy in the operations room where he had been working diligently all day, Kendra handing him a coffee.

'How's it going, young man? You've been locked away in here on your own for ages now,' Trevor said.

'There's a reason for that. This is going to be a tough job to sort out, I can tell you,' Andy replied, taking the coffee from Kendra, who winked and smiled mischievously. He lost concentration momentarily, gaining it back seconds later when he realised that she was, again, teasing him.

'Please, do tell,' Trevor said.

'First off, the people behind this are no ordinary loan sharks. I can't find anything on the system about a new or recent organisation that is loaning money on the scale we've been told about,' Andy replied.

'So, you have nothing?'

'I'm still looking, and have asked a few contacts on the dark web who are likely to know more. Also, I didn't say I found *nothing*, I managed to get something on the gangs that have been helping them.'

'Are they local, like Khan suggested?' Kendra asked.

'If you're asking whether Bethnal Green is local, then yes. But there's some confusion, because from my research, I found that a gang from south London is also involved, and they aren't so local.'

'Really? Who are they, then?' Trevor asked, confused by the revelation. It was unheard of for gangs to work together like this in London.

'We have the local boys, the Bethnal Green Boyz, twenty-odd strong, led by Imran Aziz, who is of Pakistani origin and who has been arrested previously for terrorist-related offences, supporting jihad organisations and fundraising. He's only out on the streets because of his age when he committed the offences, but he's a nasty piece of work and runs the gang with a twist on rewards. Every month there's been a report of small groups of college kids being beaten senseless by a gang matching the Bethnal Green Boyz' description, where they have used certain phrases relating to the prophet,' Andy continued.

'That doesn't sound good,' Kendra said, 'I've heard about these beatings, it's a miracle that nobody has died.'

'What about the south London crew, who are they?' Trevor asked.

'The Deptford Mafia, a Somali gang based in that part of the world and run by Raheem Abdi, numbering twenty-five or so. Known for their cold and calculating methods when dealing with their enemies, other gangs surrounding the Deptford area. Rumour has it that in order to join this gang, the prospective recruit has to take on and beat two men of a similar age and size, by any means. They achieve this by using some very innovative weapons with which they are highly skilled, such as wrist and knee protectors with spikes built in, instantly disabling their first opponent and allowing them to move quickly to the next, who they then attack with a machete or a sword. From all accounts, this lot don't give a shit about anything, and would maim their own family members to succeed.'

'How the hell do two such gangs end up working together?' Kendra asked, 'are you sure about the research?'

'Trust me, I checked more than once. The clincher was CCTV near the hotel from a week ago, when Mr Khan had his visitors. The main man and his immediate lieutenants exited a car and went straight into the hotel, leaving four henchmen to guard outside. Look at these screenshots.' Andy brought up four images on one of the monitors. 'Each image has one of the guards. Firstly, look at their features, and then look at the left arm of the two Somalis. Both are wearing strips of red cloth above their left elbow, which I'm sure is their gang mark. Any chance you can check on that when you go to work, Kendra?'

'Sure, I can do that.'

'Both gangs are involved in drugs, firearms, robberies and burglaries, so something very tempting must have happened for them to work together with loan sharks, especially out of their own areas,' Andy added.

'I'll call Rick and see if he can help with it, too,' said Kendra.

'This is highly unusual, guys, have you ever heard of an alliance like this before? It just doesn't seem likely, does it? We need to find out much more, and until we can identify the leader, the Vietnamese loan shark, we're gonna struggle,' Trevor said.

'I'm guessing they'll be looking for our hotel owner soon, which would suggest they'll be paying the place a visit, don't you think?' Kendra said.

'You're probably right, and six of our team, however competent they are, won't stand much of a chance against forty-odd gangsters, will they?' Andy said, concern written all over his face.

'I suggest we even those odds and prepare for their visit, don't you think?' Kendra asked, mischievously. 'We're going to need some of your nice shiny toys, Andy.'

'Marvellous, just what I was hoping. I'll get a few bags ready; I'll make sure there's plenty of everything for our visitors.'

'Let's meet up in an hour and take everything to the team there. I'll call Darren so he and Clive can join them there, and Jimmy and Izzy can also go there when they return from Brodie's farm. That takes it up to ten, which evens things up a little more,' Trevor said.

'Can we use some of the younger team members like we have in the past? I'm sure they can help the rest, even if it's moving stuff around for them,' Kendra said.

'Sure, but I don't want to leave the business short of staff, and they're keeping it running nicely at the moment. Maybe get Greg and Danny?'

'Greg is fully recovered now, isn't he? That was a nasty injury he got from our Albanian guests, wasn't it?' Andy said.

'He's fine now, I'm sure. The scars on his cheeks have healed nicely and are mostly hidden by his beard, now. He's kept up with his boxing with Danny, so they'd be a good fit,' Trevor said.

'Okay, I'll make the calls. See you here in an hour.' Kendra walked off.

'A nice round dozen, not including us and Rick if needed. I think we'll be able to handle them, I can't see all forty turning up, can you?' Trevor said.

'Let's hope not, and let's hope we have time to set a few surprises for them. I'll make a note of the cameras I want you to take and where to place them,' Andy said, scrabbling for a sheet of paper and a pen. 'This should be pretty challenging, Trevor.'

'Happy days, Andy. Happy days.' Trevor secretly hoped their plans would be enough to deter the gangs.

KENDRA WALKED INTO RICK WATTS' office the following morning, as she always did on workdays. As it was only two or three times a week, everyone was by now familiar with her absences and infrequent attendance, and all were aware of the early briefings with unit boss, Detective Sergeant Rick Watts, the newest member of the secret team.

'How's it going, K? Glad you decided to come in today, a few of the unit have been seconded to the Counter Terrorism Command investigation into PC Khan's murder. We could use all the help we can get,' Rick said.

'About that, we have something going on that I think is connected to Ray's murder, and it has nothing to do with terrorism,' she replied, closing the door behind her.

'What makes you say that?'

'We were approached by a close friend of Ray's father, a hotel owner in debt to a nasty loan shark operation. They're convinced that Ray was killed in order to force his father to relinquish the hotel to them. We think they used the violence during the march a few days ago and the murder outside the Jewish school to mask the real reason.'

'Bloody hell, Kendra, that's some serious shit you're talking about there. There are more than a hundred detectives looking into it as a terror attack against the school.'

'And they're wasting their time, Rick, just like the bad guys intended.'

'What the hell are we supposed to do? We can't just tell the investigation that we think they're wrong, it'll give the game up.'

'Who's been seconded to the investigation? Maybe they can plant a few seeds that will change things?'

'As luck would have it, I sent Jill and Pablo to help out. Let me call one of them and find out what they can do,' Rick said, picking up his phone.

'I need to check a couple of things out relating to a couple of gangs, Rick, all connected. You okay with me doing that before switching to other cases?'

'Yeah, go for it. Keep me in the loop and we'll catch up later,' Rick replied, giving a thumbs-up.

AT HER DESK, Kendra went through the motions of checking her messages, dealing with any minor admin issues and tasks, before reading the daily reports. She came across a couple of robberies that gave her cause to search for gangs, listing methods as the reason for the search. Knowing this would bring up many gangs in the London area, Kendra knew that nobody would question her looking into gangs and how they carried out their crimes.

'Here we go, the lovely Bethnal Green Boyz. Suspected of

more than thirty robberies, eight violent assaults, thirteen burglaries, and a dozen other crimes, they have been a busy bunch of bastards, haven't they?' she murmured.

She searched through many records, noting names, addresses, and other information that would be useful to Andy in deeper, dark web searches along with non-police databases across the southeast. After noting all she needed, she checked on several other local gangs, mimicking the searches so as not to raise any suspicions if ever an audit of her searches were conducted. When she was happy, she found the Deptford Mafia and did exactly the same, noting everything she found useful.

'I wonder what the real Mafia think about a bunch of nasty robbing bastards using their name?'

When she had finished taking notes, she went back into the list and did the same again, before making notes on the crime reports of her suspicions that the methods used pointed to suspects from a number of gangs.

And that's how to kill two birds with one stone, she thought, smiling at her achievement, knowing that other detectives would follow up and potentially be able to make arrests and solve the crimes.

A short time later she went outside and called Andy to report her findings.

'I'll take photos of the notes and send them to you, which will give you plenty to be starting with,' she said.

'Thanks, K. I'll let you know if anything pops out at me, but for now I think they're just the muscle, don't you?'

'I'm leaning that way, but I still can't figure out how they were recruited like this, to work with other gangs in different areas. We just have to keep digging and hope something comes up.'

'Catch you later, then,' he said, hanging up.

'Right then, back to the grind,' she said, walking back into the station.

'I CALLED Jill and asked her how it was all going,' Rick said later that afternoon.

'Anything exciting?'

'Not really. They've been tasked with speaking with the witnesses again, hoping that something was missed the first time around,' he said.

'Fair enough, it pays to be thorough. I've been thinking about Ray being there, though. The shooters must have known that he'd attend the school and probably planned for him to be there, right? Nothing else makes sense, which means they knew he was the local beat officer and put the call in to the school. It was always likely to be him turning up, wasn't it?'

'What are you getting at, Kendra?'

'They either knew someone who gave them that information, or they found out by other means. Is Ray mentioned on the website?'

'Let me check,' Rick said, going to the northwest area site. He typed 'Golders Green' into the search bar and waited. 'Damn, it's all here, the names of all the local beat officers, including Ray, and where they covered.'

'That was easy, wasn't it? So, they got the info from our own site and all they had to do was make a threat to the school and wait for the poor man to turn up. Damn!' Kendra cursed, shaking her head.

'Getting back to the issue, how are we going to get the investigators to look elsewhere?' Rick asked.

'It may be worth calling Jill back and cheating a little bit. Maybe pretend they're needed back here if nothing's happening there, and for her to ask about a return? Knowing Jill, she won't like that, and you can prompt her to ask the investigators questions. Maybe even get tasked with going back to the school to find out more about the death threat. Got any other ideas?'

'But how will that put them on the right track?'

'The point is that the investigation has been misdirected, and we need to find a way to get it back on track. I can't think of any other way than to get our two to help them do that,' Kendra said.

'That's fair enough, K, but we have to do it in a way that doesn't raise suspicion. Let me think about it and I'll let you know.'

'I'm guessing they've already checked the incoming call when the death threats were made, not to state the obvious,' she said.

'They did, it's an unknown number that is now dead, probably a burner phone,' Rick replied.

'Okay, let's catch up tonight, if you're free.'

'Of course, it's what I live for. And my missus thanks you kindly, too!'

4

THE GANGS

Kendra met with Trevor, Andy and Rick that evening at the factory after everyone had gone home.

'Why aren't we using the snazzy new canteen in the cube?' Andy asked as they sat at a table with their drinks.

'I don't know, to be honest,' Kendra said, 'I suppose it's habit.'

'It's cosier here, maybe not as fancy or as modern as the new place, but I like it,' Trevor added.

'It's good to see everyone again, anyway,' Rick said, 'although don't expect an invite from my missus for a while, she thinks I'm working overtime again and hates everyone.'

'We won't keep you too long, Rick, sorry about that,' Kendra said. 'Did you have any luck with Jill and Pablo?'

'I spoke with them both and they're getting frustrated with the lack of progress, much like the rest of the team there. I made a couple of subtle suggestions to get them partly on track, but I'm not sure if it'll work,' Rick replied.

'If that doesn't work, why don't we use our trusted anonymous informant?' Andy asked. 'It's worked well in the past, I don't see why it won't work now.'

'It may do, but it's wise to be careful with terrorist-related investigations as they can be much more thorough than usual. They'll likely collaborate with other agencies like MI5 and GCHQ.' Kendra was referring to the Security Service, and to Government Communications Headquarters, where the latest technology was used to detect threats and keep the country safe.

'So, we'll need to be careful what we talk about on the phone, and any other comms, you'll be surprised what they can pick up out of the ether,' Trevor added knowingly. 'We should pass that on to the rest of the team, too.'

'I'll stick to landlines from work when I'm speaking with Jill, let me see what I can do tomorrow,' Rick said.

'So, what do we know that's new?' Kendra asked, turning to Andy.

'Well, thanks to the info you sent me earlier, I managed to dig up some useful additional intel on the gangs involved.'

'Great, what can you tell us?'

'As you know, our visitors from south of the river are the Deptford Mafia, led by the lovely Raheem Abdi. In addition to what I found on the dark web, Kendra's intel allowed me to list what I believe to be the entire gang, all twenty-four of them, including two in prison. The remaining twenty-two live within a small area centred around the Pepys Estate in Deptford. I have all their names, addresses, many of their phone numbers, and seven cars registered to them, but expect there'll be some that aren't. I did some checks on the phones going back a month and noticed an interesting pattern.'

'What's that, mate?' Rick asked, impressed with the intelligence so far, 'and more to the point, why weren't you this diligent when you worked for me?'

'I was more than diligent, you just never noticed!' Andy grinned. 'Now, if I can carry on, oh ex-boss of mine?'

'Rock on, mate!' Rick laughed.

'In the past month, the phones we have for this gang have been focused around a very small area in west London, with the occasional blip where they migrate back to Deptford, so my guess is they visit home occasionally and now work in this area of North Acton, close to the infamous Hanger Lane gyratory. It's called Victoria Industrial Estate, just off the A40. There's a Travelodge hotel on the site, and my guess is that our friends from Deptford are based there while they are working for their new masters.'

'That's a good start, we'll do some digging and see if we can get some of your tiny cameras installed,' Trevor said.

'It gets better,' Andy continued, 'our friends the Bethnal Green Boyz are all based in that area, too. There's nineteen of them in the gang, but three are in prison. I have all their names, addresses, and phone numbers, along with four cars and a van. Both gangs are based in this estate now, so whatever has got them working together must be something pretty damned special.'

'I suppose it makes it easier to keep an eye on them if they're all in one place,' Trevor said, 'but that's a lot of nasty people concentrated in one small area. We're good, but taking on thirty-eight lunatics and however many the Vietnamese have in number is going to be tough.'

'We took care of two hundred Triad nutters before, didn't we?' Andy said. 'Why can't we do the same here?'

'Because that was a serious national security issue, and we had some pretty good allies to help us, Andy. I doubt the

Special Boat Squadron and Three Commando Brigade will come and help us against some loan sharks and a bunch of street hoodlums,' Kendra said.

'Maybe we can call on a few other friends,' Trevor pondered. 'Leave that one with me, we may be able to get some help from an old colleague of mine.'

'Okay, so we've managed to find out who is supporting the main man, but we don't know who that is yet, do we?' Kendra said, again turning to Andy.

'No, I have nothing except for some dodgy CCTV footage. We need new intel if we're going to identify the boss.'

'I guess we plan for that, then, make that our priority,' Trevor said. 'I'm heading to the hotel with Kendra to take the kit over, we can plan something with the team there and hope our little wannabe gangsters lead us to the end of the rainbow.'

THE REST of the team were all in place and settled at Khan's Azure Hotel, with some taking up positions on the upper floors to keep a wary eye out for any unfriendly visitors. When Trevor and Kendra arrived with a car full of equipment and supplies, Darren, Charmaine, Zoe and the twins were waiting in reception for them.

'I hope you brought snacks,' Amir said as soon as they walked in. 'We're all starving here, boss.'

'Don't listen to him, we ordered pizza and ice cream, so we're well-fed, thanks,' Mo replied, nudging his twin.

'What goodies have you brought for us, then?' Charmaine asked, rubbing her hands expectantly.

'There's a bunch of cameras that Andy wants you to place

in specific areas, just remember to check in with him so he can activate them,' Trevor said.

'There's also some extra toys we'll probably need, there's almost forty of the yobs, maybe more, so if they come mob-handed it'll give us a chance to keep them at bay,' Kendra added.

'Darren, you take this box and place everything near all four entry points,' Trevor said, handing over a large box to the Walsall boxer. 'You can set them up tonight after we leave and only remove them when someone needs to leave the hotel. We have brought extra food to avoid ordering takeaways and harming the poor delivery drivers.'

'Will do,' Darren said, smirking as he regarded the contents. 'Plus, Mr Khan said we can help ourselves to food in the kitchen, so we'll be fine.'

'Excellent; crack on, then, mate. Charmaine, you and Zoe take these two boxes and set them up at each stairwell up to and including the third floor,' Trevor continued, pointing to two other boxes, 'the containers are full and ready for deployment.'

'Amir, this is the box with the cameras. There's a piece of paper in there that Andy asked to pass on, so you know where to set them up. You'll need to do some climbing, which is why you're the best person for the job,' Kendra said, 'and then call Andy to activate them correctly. Most of them will need setting up outside, so you may need someone to help you.'

'Okey dokey,' Amir said, picking up the box and whistling as he walked away.

'That leaves one large item that we saved for last,' Trevor said, looking over at a solid wooden door lying on the floor, complete with frame.

'That one you'll need to explain,' Mo said, scratching his head.

'Don't worry, you'll like that one the best.' Kendra giggled.

'Okay, let's get to work,' Trevor said, 'make sure someone is keeping watch in case they come tonight.'

'We have plenty of people on the lookout, don't worry,' Mo said, lifting the door up at one end.

'Prop it up next to reception on the opposite side of the office door,' Trevor said.

Knowing better than to ask, Mo did as he was told and picked the heavy door up.

'Bloody hell, what's this thing made of?' he asked, barely managing to move it.

'It's a thing of wonder, that,' Trevor said, 'a solid wooden door, like the ones they used to make back in the day.'

It took much longer than expected but Mo finally made it to the wall and propped the heavy door against it.

'Get someone to help you hold it in place against the wall and then drill eight holes, three in each side and two at the top of the frame, where it's been marked. When you've done that, drill into the wall and use the Rawlplugs and screws that I've put in the drill bag. When you've screwed it to the wall, use the brown plastic plugs in the other bag to hide the screws, and then you're done,' Trevor said.

'Wait, you want me to screw a door to a concrete wall? What the hell for?'

'Because I want to see how long it'll take them to try to break it down, it'll be hilarious!' Trevor laughed.

'Won't they just use the other door?' Mo asked, seeing an obvious solution.

'No, because we're going to use the large bookshelf in Mr Khan's office to hide that door. They may find it eventually, but we can hide it for now, and screw it to the wall to make it more difficult.'

'I'd best get the drill ready again then, eh?' Mo asked, 'and by the way, I'm very glad we're on the same side!'

It was late by the time the team had finished the preparations. Kendra checked with Andy to confirm the cameras were active and Trevor went round once to check everything was in situ, giving guidance where required and offering encouragement all round.

'Remember, your safety is the priority, so don't put yourself at risk unnecessarily. Do as much as you can and get the hell out of there when the risk is too high, okay?'

'Don't worry, Trevor, we're all aware of the danger and know when to retreat, we'll be fine,' Charmaine said.

'Good. Call us as soon as you have contact, we'll make our way over and support from the perimeter in any way we can,' Kendra added.

Once assured the team was ready, they left and made their way back to the factory, where they would stay the night, knowing that was all they could do for the time being.

'It won't be long now, love,' Trevor said, 'my guess is that they're making plans as we speak. They'll come tonight or tomorrow, and now that we're ready for them we can prep the factory for our soon-to-be guests.'

'Okay, I'll just pop and see Andy and then join you to check the rooms,' she replied, referring to the reinforced rooms at the rear of the factory where they kept *guests* until deciding where to move them.

Andy was monitoring the live feeds from the hotel, twiddling a pen in his free hand, when Kendra walked into the operations room. As ever, he looked somewhat dashing with his eyepatch and slightly unkempt hair, and definitely relaxed in his role within the team. He was enjoying their adventure greatly.

'How goes it, Detective March?' he said, smiling when he saw her. 'Are our colleagues ready to rock and roll?'

'They most certainly are, Mr Pike. Our visitors are in for a treat when they turn up, that's for sure.' She stroked his arm affectionately as she brushed by him. Both wanted so much more, but for now, they restricted themselves to the occasional reminder, a gentle touch here, some suggestive flirting there.

Andy smiled and shook his head slightly, knowing it was part of the odd game they played.

'That's good. I've got most of the cameras on infra-red outside the hotel and I'm also watching their phones and seeing if there's any movement towards the Azure, so we should have a heads-up when an attack is imminent,' he said, as she sat opposite him.

'You understand more than most that this lot needs taking down, Andy. They killed a fellow officer in the line of duty, so they deserve the best form of justice we can give,' she said, the defiance in her voice evident.

'I get that, K. Hopefully we've enough experience now to get the evidence we need, but you know as well as I do that these criminals cover their tracks very well. If we're going to see justice dispensed, then it's more likely to come from us than the courts. Just as long as you're aware and comfortable with that.'

'Oh, I am, don't you worry. These bastards will burn in hell if I have anything to do with it!'

'Hold onto your hat, young lady, because it seems we have some movement. A dozen phones are on the move in four clumps, so likely four vehicles. All from the Deptford Mafia crew, all now on the A406 North Circular Road heading east. You should let the team know they'll have company in about thirty minutes,' Andy said, pointing at one of the monitors showing the phones' locations.

'I'll call everyone now,' she said, heading out of the room to let Trevor know, and dialled Charmaine.

'They're on the way, Charmaine, probably a dozen in four different vehicles with an ETA of thirty minutes. We'll get there around about the same time, so I'll call when we're close,' she said.

'Received and understood, we're ready,' Charmaine said, and hung up.

'And so it begins,' Kendra said, as she went in search of Trevor.

5

ATTACK!

Trevor and Kendra parked the van and were in place just minutes before the four Deptford Mafia cars turned up, and quickly hid behind the bin stores next to the car park. The cars stopped close to the hotel entrance and three young men got out of each. Some carried baseball bats, others carried butterfly knives that they opened and closed as they walked with purpose. Kendra saw at least two handguns, tucked into the back of the gangsters' trousers. She looked at her father and nodded, knowing what they needed to do once the men were inside.

One man stood ahead of the other eleven and Trevor knew that he was looking at gang leader Raheem Abdi, an imposing figure, wearing a leather jacket and a chunky gold chain around his neck. Worryingly, he had a rapier-type sword strapped to his back, the hilt within easy reach. As the group reached the main entrance, Abdi indicated for two of his men to double around the back. He indicated to another to get the door. The subordinate grabbed the door handle and pulled, only to find it locked.

'It's locked, but feels loose,' the man said, pulling harder.

What they were unaware of was that Darren had fixed a small bolt on the inside, one that would break easily when pulled, and that was exactly what happened.

'Crap security for a crap hotel, eh?' Abdi said to his laughing men. 'Go. Find the cheap bastard and bring him to me. It's time to take a hand.' He reached up to feel the hilt of the sword, looking forward to using it soon.

The first man entered through the doorway into the darkened reception area. He could see outlines, thanks to the lighting in front of the hotel, enough for him to get his bearings and to see where everything was. He stepped forward, his left foot landing directly on one of the dozens of caltrops the team had left behind as the first surprise. The man, Ahmed, screamed in agony as one of the spikes on the four-pronged heavy-gauge metal device embedded itself deep in his foot. Unsteady on his right foot, he tumbled over and screamed again as two more caltrops hit home, one in his upper arm and another in his upper thigh. The pain was excruciating, and, realising that moving too much would cause him more pain, he remained still on the ground, yelling for help. One of his friends, Ali, had also entered the hotel and was going through similar pain but had managed to remain standing as his right foot was impaled by a single caltrop.

Abdi immediately stopped anyone else from going in.

'Watch yourselves, the bastard has left us some surprises. Get your phones out and shine them on the floor, I want to see what he has done,' he said.

The phone torches illuminated enough to see the caltrops scattered around the entrance.

'Bilan, move those things before anyone else gets hurt.

Yusuf and Farah, go and help Ahmed and Ali,' he ordered, looking beyond his injured men and into the hotel.

He could see the doors to the two stairwells, one on each side of the reception desk, along with two lifts on the far side and a door that he believed led to the hotel offices between them. Once the wounded and the spikes were moved out of the way, he indicated for his men to take positions by the stairwells and the door, but not to move just yet. He guessed correctly that the lifts were likely to have been deactivated, and dismissed them as an option. When they were in position, he and the remainder of his crew entered cautiously. He slowly unsheathed the rapier on his back and held it by his side, the feel of the hilt comforting to him.

Kendra saw the gang's initial attempt and nodded to Trevor that it was time for them to move. They left their hiding place and moved quickly at a crouch towards the four cars. They each had a GPS tag, which they quickly placed on the inside of the rear bumpers, using a dollop of mastic to keep them in place. Within seconds they moved away, closer to the hotel entrance, where they saw the two injured men on the ground, leaning against the wall.

'Will they do?' Kendra whispered.

'Yes, but let's wait for the rest of them to move farther in,' Trevor said.

Inside, Raheem looked around to see that his men were in position. Four were covering the stairwells, two at each, and three were covering the locked door. The stairwell men had their weapons ready, mainly baseball bats and knives. Of the three covering the locked door, one had a crowbar and the other baseball bats. They were ready.

'Go!' Raheem shouted, 'find him!'

He then called the two men covering the other entrances and told them to gain entry.

'There is no other way out.' Raheem smirked as he saw his men attacking the doors. 'We have him.'

The two stairwell doors had been locked. Unlike those at the main entrance, the locks were more robust and required much more effort. The men took turns to kick them, and Raheem could see, despite the poor lighting, that the doorframes were shaking from the impact. Turning his attention to the door leading to the offices, he could see they were having less of an impact. The man using the crowbar tried several points without success, so the other men took turns to kick at it. Unlike the other doors, Raheem couldn't see the frame shaking, raising his suspicions. He walked over to the trio.

'He must be in there; the door looks more secure than the others, try smashing the middle with the crowbar, do something different, but keep trying!' he shouted to his men.

He watched as they continued to batter the door, which was now starting to splinter in places from the impact of the crowbar. Raheem could see that it was a solid door and would take more time. He walked back to the others to see if they had made progress, and heard a shout from one of his men as he approached.

'We're through!'

'Go, but be cautious!' Raheem shouted. He heard the other team call out and moved to them and saw the other stairwell door had also been breached.

'You too; go, but look for more of those spike things!'

The men cautiously entered the hallways. One had stairs leading down to the boiler and laundry rooms. The other had stairs leading down to storerooms. They would search the basement later; nobody could escape without passing reception. Both stairwells had signs indicating the restaurant and conference rooms on the first floor, with bedrooms on all floors thereafter. As the hotel had twelve floors, it would take some time to search, but Raheem was in no rush.

The first duo cautiously climbed towards the first floor, weapons at the ready, as their eyes adjusted to the darker stairwell. There was some moonlight, the windows helping slightly, but not quite enough for them to feel comfortable. They couldn't see any danger on the steps leading up, which gave them a little more confidence and so increased their pace slightly. They soon reached the first-floor landing and the locked door leading to the restaurant and conference rooms. Each man grabbed a handle and pulled with all their might, enough to force open the door, small pieces from the lock scattering around them.

Neither of them had realised they were standing in some sort of liquid until they went from the tiled landing floor into the carpeted hall. Only then did they realise something was not as it should be, their feet sticking to the carpet and making it difficult to move.

'What the hell, bro?' one man said, 'what's going on?'

'I don't know, man, there's something on the carpet, like glue, I think.'

Before moving forward, they used the torches on their phones to light the way. The few seconds that took made it more difficult to move, the adhesive taking effect and slowing them down significantly.

'I don't like this, we should go back,' one man said as he laboured towards the first set of doors.

'I don't like it either, but I'd rather step on a spike than have Raheem thrash the living daylights out of me,' his friend said.

Both men nodded as they got to the double doors and opened them cautiously, stepping into the large restaurant area. Despite better lighting, it was eerie being in a place that was normally a hive of activity. They continued to walk, still slowed by the glue on their feet, to which they paid more attention as they quickly realised they'd eventually come to a stop.

'I think we'll have to take our shoes off,' one man said.

'We should be alright,' his comrade replied, 'there's no spikes in here. Just be mindful of anything else that might be on the floor.'

They both removed their shoes, tying the laces together, the shoes now hanging from their belts for later. They continued slowly, freed from the sticky floor and moving confidently through the restaurant. They approached the island in the middle, unaware of movement behind them. By the time they realised something was amiss, it was too late.

Just as they reached the island, a dark figure rose from behind it, wearing a mask similar to those that soldiers wore, and holding what looked like a spray gun, the kind that was used to spray garden fences. This stopped them in their tracks and before they could react, the figure pulled the trigger and unleashed a liquid that engulfed them both, covering their faces and torsos with a thick, glutinous mix that seemed to glow orange in the dim light.

Spluttering and temporarily blinded, they both turned away from their attacker in an attempt to flee, both trying to clear the fluid from their eyes, not realising there was another masked figure behind them, who pulled the trigger on their spray gun and covered them with a similar liquid, this time one that seemed to glow green. They didn't see that there were now caltrops all over the floor ahead, which they now ran into as they tried to escape their attackers. Within two steps, they were both on the floor in agony as the spikes did their job. Their downfall had taken a matter of seconds.

The two masked figures calmly strode over to them, clearing a path for themselves. They took the Deptford visitors' weapons and rifled through their pockets and removed phones, knives and money, placing everything into Faraday bags to prevent any signals getting through or being tracked.

Using heavy-duty zip ties, the two men were restrained at the ankles and wrists.

'This may hurt,' one of the masked figures said, pulling two of the spikes from one man and a single one from the other.

Both men screamed in pain. Only when they had stopped did their captors wipe some of the liquid away and cover their mouths with duct tape, rendering them silent. They were then dragged to one side, where their bleeding feet were quickly bandaged after antiseptic was sprayed on.

'If you try and do anything stupid, we won't be so kind next time.'

Both men nodded, knowing they weren't likely to escape any time soon.

'Two down,' Charmaine told Darren as she called it in.

IN THE SECOND STAIRWELL, the other two men had also made it to the first floor and had entered the first conference room, having struggled with the same problem as their comrades. They hadn't taken their shoes off, unlike their friends, and had struggled until they were met by two masked attackers who covered them with the same sticky liquid that hampered their movement and temporarily blinded them. Fluorescent purple and glutinous red fluid were the preferred choices in this instance.

Unlike their colleagues, it wasn't caltrops that brought them down but thirty thousand volts from the team's trusted Axion Taser 7 guns. Both men were quickly incapacitated, stripped of all weaponry and personal effects, and bound by the ankles and wrists, their mouths covered with duct tape. They were pulled to one side, out of sight, to await their fate.

'Two down first floor,' Jimmy told Darren, calling it in.

'Thanks, Jimmy, that's four down inside, two injured men down outside, six to go. One of you stay with our guests and the other go and help Clive and Martin with the rear entrances,' Darren said.

'Will do, I'll send Izzy and stay here.'

KENDRA AND TREVOR could see that Raheem and three of his cronies were focused on the fake door, and so moved swiftly towards the two injured men, who had limped over to one of the cars and sat inside, nursing their injuries.

'Okay, remember what we discussed, Dad?'

'Yes, yes, I remember, daughter,' Trevor replied.

They moved towards the car, a two-year-old silver Vauxhall Astra, where the two men occupied the front seats. Splitting up, Kendra went to the driver's side and Trevor to the other, crouching down out of sight. When they were both in position, Trevor whistled.

Kendra then stood and opened the driver's door, surprising the hell out of the man sitting there.

'Hello, do you have the time?' she asked innocently.

Both men stared at her in shock.

Kendra's entrance was Trevor's signal to open the passenger door.

'Hello, boys,' he said, as he sprayed the passenger with a red dye laced with pepper spray, temporarily blinding him. Kendra did the same with the driver, stepping back quickly so as not to be affected by the incapacitant. They then closed both doors and waited a few seconds for the men to be completely disoriented.

'Close your eyes and hold your breath when you drag him out,' Trevor said.

They both did so as they opened the doors and dragged the occupants out, both spluttering and gasping for air. It wasn't as toxic as CS spray, but it was useful as the effects were much shorter. They dragged the men farther out of sight. Working quickly, the pair quickly secured the two men and rifled through their pockets for phones and personal effects, putting everything into the trusted Faraday bags for security.

'How long should we wait?' Kendra asked.

'I'd go now, while they're busy. They won't be getting through that door any time soon!'

Kendra reached into the Faraday bag and removed a set of Audi A4 car keys. It was for the blue car closest to the hotel, within sight of Raheem and his men. It was a new model, which the gang leader had arrived in.

'I'll go and get it,' she said. 'I'll meet you here so we can take these two away.'

'Okay, just remember to turn the headlights off before you start it, in case,' Trevor said.

Kendra nodded before making her way quickly to the Audi.

She took a quick look to check the coast was clear before getting into the driver's seat. She saw the headlights were not in automatic mode, so they wouldn't come on. She turned the engine on and slowly reversed towards Trevor and their captives. Eventually the Audi was out of view, and they were able to bundle one of the men into the boot without too much fuss, before placing the other in the Astra.

'We can park them close to the van and come back,' she said, getting back into the driver's seat. It took them a few minutes to take both cars away from the scene before returning.

'I heard from Darren: they have six of the men safely secured, which just leaves the four trying to smash down the fake door.' Trevor grinned.

'When do you want to take them down?' she asked.

'It depends, let's see how long they take in there and what they decide to do when they realise their friends won't be joining them.'

'They'll be without two of their cars,' Kendra added, 'which will make Stav very happy.' Stav would be stripping the cars for parts very quickly and adding to their ongoing account with him as their vehicle supplier.

'Hang on, something's happening inside,' Trevor said.

RAHEEM WAS PERPLEXED by why it was taking so long to smash through the door, and told his men to stop. The door was now badly damaged, splinters and chunks of wood covering the floor around them, but was somehow still secure in its frame. He saw that a small hole had been made where his man had been attacking the same spot over and over. Shining his torch at the hole, he swore out loud as he realised what had happened.

'What the fuck? There's a concrete wall behind this door!'

Looking around, he noticed that none of his men had returned. He dialled a number, waiting for an answer that never came. He tried two more numbers to no avail, before realising that they were no longer the attackers, but the prey.

'We must go! Now!' he shouted to his three remaining men.

They headed for the entrance, looking around them warily, two of them with their handguns out and Raheem with his sword. He swore again when he realised his two injured men were nowhere to be seen and that two cars were missing. He had come to the hotel thinking it would be an easy task but now understood he'd been taken for a fool.

That would not happen again.

'Get the cars!' he yelled.

His men were able to start the two cars and he got into one quickly.

'Go, quick!'

Both cars drove away at speed, leaving behind eight missing men and a pair of valuable cars.

TREVOR AND KENDRA had quickly realised that taking on the remaining four men would not be a good idea, in light of the handguns and the sword.

'We've done well, and they will lead us to their boss soon enough,' Trevor said.

'Let's call in and see where we're at,' Kendra said.

They called Darren and Charmaine and confirmed that everyone was safe and well and that the remaining six men were incapacitated and waiting transport to the factory.

'Let's go and get the van,' Trevor said, 'and we'll put our two friends from the Audi in there, too.'

Kendra called Andy with an update.

'The cameras worked well, I saw everything and was able to tell Izzy and Darren where the two men at the rear were,' he said. 'And I'm now tracking the two cars back to where they're hiding.'

'That's good, thanks. I know they're likely to go back to the hotel in the industrial estate, but we may get lucky, and they take us to the big boss soon,' Kendra replied.

'Okay. The rooms are ready for our new guests, so I'll see you soon.'

'So far, so good,' Kendra told Trevor.

'Let's not count our chickens just yet, love, we know how quickly things can go wrong!'

THE TWINS TOOK and drove the now-empty cars to Stav's garage not too far from the factory, while the team loaded the trussed prisoners into the van that Trevor had driven to the hotel. Leaving most of the team behind, with instructions to repair any damage and prepare for further attacks, he and Kendra, along with Greg and Danny, who stayed in the rear with the gang members, left for the factory.

'We could have done with a few more people with this lot,

let's get these locked up as soon as possible and come back to reinforce them,' Kendra said.

'Agreed,' said Trevor. 'I told Darren and Charmaine to think up some different traps for our friends now that they've experienced our welcome party!'

'You say that, but all they've seen is a fake door and the caltrops, they won't have a clue what happened to the rest of the men upstairs, will they?' Kendra said.

'No, but I'm sure the team will think up some inventive new ways to stop them.'

'What we need is to find the person behind this and take them all out as soon as possible so this lot can go back to their own playgrounds.'

'If only it were that easy,' Trevor said.

6

BTK

In the loading bay back at the factory, Trevor and Kendra helped Greg and Danny to unload the prisoners, dragging them one by one to their new accommodation and handcuffing them securely in place in the specially adapted secure rooms. All eight men were given instructions not to call for help or to try to escape, on pain of being tasered. Trevor gave Greg and Danny instructions and left them in charge of the guests while he and Kendra went to speak with Andy.

'Good job, guys, eight out of twelve isn't a bad start. That's gonna hurt them,' Andy said as they walked in.

'I agree, but remember: it's when things are going well that something usually comes along to screw things up. Let's not get ahead of ourselves, there's still thirty of them left, plus an unknown number of Vietnamese gangsters.'

'Anything happen while we were sorting our friends out?' Kendra asked. 'We need to get back as soon as possible in case they come back with reinforcements.'

'Actually, I have plenty to tell you,' Andy said.

The monitor showed one red light, stationary, at the Travelodge in the industrial park where the gangs were currently based. The other red light was stationary at a different location, a car park of a small, detached building on the outskirts of the industrial estate.

'What's that, then, Andy?' Trevor asked.

'That, my friend, is where our big boss is based. It used to be a hair salon supplies distributor before it was bought by Legacy Solutions, a limited company that doesn't seem to have much of an online presence. What I did find, though, was both interesting and disturbing.'

'Go on,' Trevor said.

'Legacy Solutions is owned by one Raymond Kam, born forty-three years ago in Long Island, New York. I did a deep dive into this man's background and found out that he and his family emigrated to the UK thirty-three years ago and set up home in Hounslow, west London, where Raymond's parents opened a successful Vietnamese restaurant.'

'What disturbing about that?' Kendra asked.

'I'm coming to that, don't worry. I went back a few years and found out why they had come to the UK. Raymond's father was one of the top-tier members of the notorious Born to Kill gang in New York, or BTK as they were known. They were ruthless and took no prisoners, killing rivals by the dozen and burying bodies all over the state. He was one of a handful that managed to escape a massive purge by the authorities where the main boss and the majority of members were jailed for long periods, mainly for racketeering, as there wasn't enough evidence for the multiple murders. Raymond is now running some sort of operation over here and is starting to make some big gains. This is not going to be easy, I can tell you.'

'Good job finding this info, Andy. We need to come up with a plan to stop this lot, but without having all the information, we're going to struggle. It's not going to be easy trying to defend against the gangsters at the hotel while trying to take their boss out. Any ideas?'

'I may be able to get some help, kill two birds with one stone, as it were.' Trevor winked.

'Great, because we're going to need all the help we can get,' she replied.

'We'll catch up later, Andy. Crack on with whatever you can, and we'll update as and when,' Trevor said, patting him on the back. 'We need to get back to the team.'

'I'll ask some of my mysterious friends on the dark web if they know anything about Mr Kam.' With that, Andy waved them off.

He sighed as he found himself, once again, alone in the operations room.

It's a good job I love doing this, otherwise I'd swear they were trying to stop me from having some fun out there, he thought.

BEFORE LEAVING FOR THE HOTEL, Trevor and Kendra raided the storerooms for supplies. Having seen that the opposition would likely arrive in numbers, the last thing they needed was to run out.

'Let's take these as well, just in case things go wrong,' Kendra said, taking coils of rope down from the shelves. 'After all, you're the one who told me there should always be an escape route.'

'Yes, I did, and that is why you should speak to Rick and

see whether he can send someone on the hurry-up if it all kicks off,' said Trevor.

'That will be tough to explain, won't it? What will he tell his superiors?'

'He'll have to come up with a legitimate reason, maybe an informant called, or an anonymous passer-by saw people with guns heading towards the hotel, I'm sure he can think of something. To be honest, I doubt we'll need it, but it's good to have that extra back-up.'

'Okay, I'll call him when we're on the way, I need to update him anyway,' Kendra said.

'Right, I think we have everything, let's go.'

They loaded the van with the equipment and set off for the hotel. Kendra called Rick with a progress report.

'That's great, K, now we know who's behind this, it'll help greatly,' he said.

'Yeah, but we're no nearer to knowing why this is all happening, are we?'

'I guess not, but one step at a time, Detective, you should remember that from week one of your training!' Rick laughed.

'Thanks for the reminder, boss. Dad thinks we should have a back-up plan with you in place in case it all goes to rat shit. Got any ideas how you can get us some help if we need it quickly? Dad reckons an anonymous passer-by or an informant.'

'I don't want to keep using the informant angle, K, what will help is if we use a burner phone and call it in that way. Anonymous, and through the correct channel. That way, I'll most likely get a call to be informed anyway.'

'That'll do it. Okay, I'll use one of our burners and bin it afterwards,' she said. 'I'll let you know if anything else happens on our end, is there anything going on with Jill and Pablo?'

'No, nothing yet, but they're getting to the point where they are starting to doubt the terrorist theory, which is moving in the right direction. If we can get some evidence to help with that later, then the poor PC's death can be avenged.'

'Amen to that. We'll certainly try. Catch you later, Rick,' Kendra said, ending the call.

'Right then, let's go set some more traps,' she said to herself.

ON THE WAY back to the hotel, Trevor decided to call for some assistance.

'Blimey, that was quick,' Mike Romain said, 'I thought you'd keep us waiting for at least a month.'

'Well, since you were so kind to offer your services when you came to our grand opening, I thought it would be too good an opportunity to waste,' said Trevor.

'Received and understood, my friend. So, tell me what you need.'

'We have a situation, where we have a job that is too big for my team to handle alone. We have two areas that need covering; one we can handle, but the other, more sensitive one needs some finesse that I know your surveillance team can provide.'

'Go on.'

'The subject I need you to follow is the son of a New York gangster who escaped arrest back in the nineties and came to the UK. This subject is now running some vicious operations and is killing people to achieve his objectives. Make no mistake, Mike, this guy is gonna be tough to follow and even tougher to get evidence from. Think you can handle it?' Trevor had his fingers firmly crossed.

'Let me tell you something you don't know, old friend. My team has followed some of the most surveillance-conscious criminals you can ever imagine and has never been blown out. Trust me, Trev, we can do this.'

'That's great. We'll sort the business side of things when we meet up. When can you get back to our place?'

'I can pop over tomorrow.'

'One thing I have to ask, Mike, is that you may need to bend the surveillance laws a little to achieve your objective. It won't be for court or anything like that, and whatever evidence you get will be used anonymously, so nobody in your team will ever have to justify their actions. If you're good with that, then we'll do a lot of business together, I promise you.'

'I always said the law was an ass, Trev, even you'll remember me whinging about that,' Mike said.

'That I do, which is why we're having this conversation, mate. Hopefully your team will have the same mindset.'

'Don't worry about my team, Trev, they're the best and the most discreet I've ever had the pleasure of working with. I'll catch up with you tomorrow, okay?'

'Okay, mate, see you then.'

'That sounded like it went well,' Kendra said as they drove back towards the hotel.

'I knew he was right for this sort of work as soon as he agreed to come to our opening. He is going to be a great asset, K, imagine how much we can do with a top-notch surveillance team that can actually gather intelligence and evidence on the move, instead of having to rely on those tiny cameras of Andy's.'

'You'll get no argument from me,' Kendra said, 'but Andy may take offence, especially since those cameras have worked so well for us!'

'Nah, he'll be fine. We'll just tell him it'll mean he can come out on site more often, he'll love us for it.'

'I'm starting to think you know him better than I do!' Kendra laughed.

'I learn quick, daughter, haven't you noticed that about me yet?'

'I guess I have a lot to learn still, right?'

'There will be plenty of time for that, love, but for now we need to get back and make sure our people are properly protected from what's coming their way,' Trevor said grimly, knowing that the next attack would be much more brutal on the team.

TREVOR HAD one last call to make before they reached the hotel. He had to stifle a laugh before he connected, knowing what was to come.

'How's it going, Brodie? I hope you're treating your guests well,' he said.

'I can almost hear you laughing, you sadistic git,' Brodie said. 'As it happens, we're having the best time here, so you can stop your grinning. Noora and Anika have been helping with the cooking, so we've had some of the best curries and sweets we've ever had, and Kamal has been helping me with the greenhouse. That man has got green fingers, I tell you.'

'I'm happy to hear that, Brodie, but how have they really been?'

'I won't lie, there's been a lot of tears, but keeping busy has helped them a lot. Noora has confided in my missus quite a lot, and their daughter Anika has been helping the farm crew. They're a lovely family, Trevor, so I take back what I said about you after we last spoke.'

'Why? What did you say about me?'

'Oh, you don't have to worry about that now. So, what are you calling for? I'm sure it's not to see how I am coping, is it?'

'No, I actually called to speak to Mr Khan. Is he there?'

'Hang on, I'll get him.'

The phone went silent for a few seconds before Brodie came back on.

'Here he is. I'll pass you over, but just because things are good here doesn't mean you're squirming out of our deal, you hear?'

'I'm good for it, Brodie, so stop fretting, now put Mr Khan on!' Trevor laughed.

'Hello?'

'Hello, Mr Khan. How are you all settling in at the farm? I hope Brodie is treating you well.'

'He has been a gentleman, so thank you for making my family safe. What can I do for you?'

'Mr Khan, the gangs made an attempt to look for you here last night. We managed to stop them, but we think they'll be coming back tonight or tomorrow. I wanted your permission to raid your basement supplies so we can prepare some surprises for them. Is that okay?'

'You take whatever you need, Mr Trevor, I only care about my family now, the hotel is a distant second.'

'You'll get your hotel back, Mr Khan, I promise, so don't

give up on it just yet. There may be a little damage, but we'll be able to help you fix that, and hopefully these people will not be bothering you again,' Trevor said.

'Thank you; again, I appreciate it greatly.'

'It's our pleasure. I'll be in touch when it's safe to come back, but in the meantime please don't leave the farm or call anyone with your mobile phones, okay?'

'They've been turned off since we got here and will remain so until we return, you have my word.'

'Thank you and goodnight,' Trevor replied, hanging up.

'What's that about the basement? What are you up to, Dad?' Kendra was mystified by the request her father had just made.

'We need all the help we can get, so it's time to get sneaky with our surprises.'

7

REINFORCEMENTS

It was very late by the time they returned to the hotel, and most of the team were now resting. With no shortage of comfortable rooms, and plenty of food and other supplies, spirits were still high. Mo had overseen the restoration of some of the traps and tweaked some of the others, mixing it up a little, so it was now a waiting game.

'Any indications when they'll be returning?' Charmaine asked.

'Not yet. Andy confirmed that the remaining gang members are mostly stationary in the hotel at the industrial park, so hopefully it won't be tonight. Which is just as well, because there'll be more of them next time, and they'll probably be more heavily armed. We need to beef the security and add a few more surprises for them early tomorrow, okay?'

'No problem, boss, anything particular in mind?' Amir asked.

'Funny you mention it, Amir, but I thought we'd spice things up a bit... literally,' Trevor said, handing over a bag filled with pepper spray in purpose-built spray canisters with a reach of five metres.

'Cool, it's about time we used these,' Amir said.

'Just be sure everyone on the team wears the full kit: masks, goggles, ballistic vests, the lot, I don't want anyone taking any chances,' Kendra added.

'Don't worry, I'll make sure they do,' Amir said, heading off to hand the canisters out.

'Darren, I want you to add these to each entrance to make it as difficult as possible for them to enter next time,' Trevor said, handing over a box of heavy-duty bolts along with a bag of plastic door wedges.

'This should leave them vulnerable outside for a bit longer than they'll like,' Darren replied, taking the boxes. 'Have you got anything in mind for them, then?'

'Does a bear shit in the woods?' Kendra laughed. 'I could literally hear his mind ticking on the way over!'

'Mr Khan has kindly given us permission to use whatever we need from the hotel, including the boiler room and the laundrette. The surprise I have in mind for them outside will not be very pleasant,' said Trevor.

'Ooh, this is going to be a lot of fun,' Charmaine said, rubbing her hands together.

'Don't count on that. This lot are a different cut than what we're used to, they don't give a fig about anyone, even their own lot, so you'll need to have your wits about you.'

'Don't worry, Kendra, it's just my way of dealing with danger, I try and make light of it. Not everyone approves, but it works for me.'

'Then have at it!' Kendra laughed.

'We've brought a few more boxes of replacement goo, as

you like to call it, and a few more tasers, just in case,' Trevor said.

'Great, I'll get these in place tonight and we can start on reinforcing the hotel tomorrow,' Mo said.

'I need to meet someone at the factory tomorrow, so I'll join you after that and cover the perimeter like before, with Kendra.'

'Okay, I guess we'll see you tomorrow, then,' Mo said, waving them off.

'I think it's time for us to head on home, don't you?' Kendra said, yawning.

'Agreed, there's a lot to do tomorrow and not much time in between,' Trevor replied.

'No rest for the wicked, eh?'

ON THE WAY to Kendra's flat, they received a call from Andy.

'Everything okay back there?' Kendra asked, 'any change?'

'No change, they're all still cooped up at the hotel. I did find something interesting that you need to know about, though.'

'What's that?'

'Someone's been offering SA80s on the dark web,' he said, 'a lot of them.'

'Shit, is there any chance you can trace them?' Kendra asked.

'Only if you count a meeting with them tomorrow.'

Trevor jumped in. 'What are you talking about?'

'I made a snap decision and put myself forward as a

buyer. I'm meeting them tomorrow at noon to look at a batch of the rifles.'

'I don't know whether that's a good thing or not,' Kendra said. 'Did you actually speak with them or was it all online chat?'

'It was all chat. They know neither what I sound like or look like,' Andy replied.

'That's a relief, because I'll be going to the meeting instead. I'll be more believable than you. You look like a yuppie that hasn't had a shower in a couple of days,' Trevor said, 'not the illegal gun-buying kind of criminal they'll be expecting.'

'Ouch, that was a low blow, I thought I looked like a great criminal, what with this eyepatch. Plus, I'm trying to grow my hair out, that's all. And for your information, I showered yesterday.'

'Are you sure about this, Dad?' Kendra asked.

'I've done this many times, love, remember? It's what I was recruited for by army intelligence. I look the part and I play it well, so I'm a natural choice. Where's the meet, Andy?'

'I wanted it to be somewhere public and open, so I chose the Rose gallery upper car park at the Bluewater Shopping Centre. I told them I'd be in a silver Mercedes, like the one we have in the back here. Does that work for you?'

'Good job, that man. What are they coming in?' Trevor asked.

'A blue Land Rover Discovery. There will be two of them, so you know.'

'Okay, good. I'll need some of your fancy microphone gear and a GPS tag, so I may need you to come and help me with that, love.'

'Count me in, Dad. I'll get there much earlier and find

somewhere suitable to wait until they turn up. The Land Rover should be easy to attach a tag to.'

'Okay, that's settled, then. Let's all get some rest now, we have a lot going on tomorrow,' Trevor said.

'Darn, so close,' Andy said, grinning at the missed opportunity to get involved.

MIKE ROMAIN MET with Trevor and Kendra first thing in the morning in the canteen of the new building, the cube.

'So, talk to me, Trevor,' he said as they sat down with their drinks.

'Since we spoke, there's been a bit of a development that may require two separate follows. Do you have the capability to cover both?' Trevor asked.

'Not effectively, no. If we split the team, we'd compromise both follows, so we should stick to one and go back another time if the opportunity arises for the other,' Mike said.

'Then we have a bit of a dilemma. Before we give you the info on both jobs, I want to clarify that what we do can get us into a lot of trouble if caught, so you need to be sure about getting involved, Mike.'

'Mate, if you want me to sign an NDA, I'd be happy to do so,' he said, referring to a non-disclosure agreement, typically signed when business ventures were being discussed.

'I'm good if you're good, Mike. And to be clear, we'll pay your usual daily rate plus ten percent at the end of each separate operation once you have invoiced us, right?' Kendra said.

'That's generous of you, thank you, I'm more than happy with those terms.'

The two old colleagues shook on the deal.

'Welcome aboard, Mike. Your mission, should you choose to accept it, is one of the following,' Trevor started. 'I've been waiting years to say that!'

He placed two folders in front of Mike, opening the first to show a photograph of Raymond Kam, the Vietnamese gangster.

'This was going to be your original target,' Kendra said, 'but we think he is someone we can come back to later.'

'This is what we'd like you to start with, to help us trace and retrieve,' Trevor continued, opening the second folder to show a picture of a box of brand new SA80 rifles, like the ones stolen from the base.

'Shit, brand new SA80s? How many?'

'Almost a hundred,' said Kendra. 'We think there's a handful on the streets of London as we speak, but whoever has them is trying very hard to sell the rest.'

'You know where they are?'

'No, but we know where some of them will be at noon today, when I go and meet with the sellers. We need you to follow them from there, at a distance, because we'll hopefully have a GPS tag on their motor, but when they stop, we'll need boots on the ground to get intel or evidence,' Trevor said.

'Okay, that's a pretty decent job for us to start our relationship with, mate. Tell me more.'

'Here's the folder with all the numbers of the missing guns, along with photos of the man we believe stole them, a disgruntled ex-navy sergeant. That's all we have for now, which is why you can help us get more. We need to get these things off the streets, Mike, they'll cause carnage if we don't,' Trevor said.

'They're a lethal bit of kit, for sure. We'll do what we can. I'll go and brief my team, and we'll look to be on plot forty-five minutes before the meet. Keep me in the loop in case anything changes, okay?'

'Cheers, Mike, we'll see you later,' Trevor said, shaking his hand again.

'Damn, I missed you and the trouble you always got into, this is so bloody typical of you, Trev!' Mike laughed on his way out.

THEY DECIDED to take two cars, just in case the car park was being watched. Kendra left first and drove directly to the ground floor car park at Bluewater, electing to walk to the nearby Rose Gallery upper car park, limiting the chances of being spotted. Arriving forty-five minutes before the scheduled meeting meant she had plenty of time to find it and check it out. Although it wasn't full, it was busy enough that there were plenty of places for her to retreat to safely in advance of the meet.

'Make sure you keep me in the loop, Andy, so I know exactly where they meet. I want to be nice and close to their car when it turns up. I imagine I won't have much time to do what I need to do,' she said.

'Don't worry, I'll have an open line with Trevor so you can listen in for yourself. Just be careful, young lady.'

'Don't worry, old man, I'll be just fine,' she joked. 'Now, I need to have another walk around just in case, so I'll catch up with you later.'

'Righty ho.'

Kendra walked around the car park, noting the exits, where the ramp was, and realised that the meet was likely to be at the far corner, farthest away from the exits to the shopping centre, where there were fewer cars. She walked there and looked around to see where she could wait; the only option was a stairwell leading down to the next level, very close to the way out.

This could be tricky, she thought, looking around to see if there was anything else.

She noticed the silver Mercedes that Trevor was driving around slowly, checking the location for himself.

It was then that Andy phoned.

'Heads-up,' he said, 'I managed to get into the CCTV system and there is a blue Land Rover Discovery, two up, heading towards the car park now. I have an index of *Romeo-Mike-seven-zero-tango-tango-Juliet*. It's heading for the roundabout, where they'll take the slip road to the car park ramp. I reckon you have less than a minute.'

'Damn, they're fifteen minutes early,' Kendra said, as she started running towards the busier end of the car park to look for cover. 'Tell Dad there's not much cover in the far corner and ask him to move to the adjacent corner, where I can use cars to hide behind.'

'Will do.'

The silver Mercedes picked up pace and drove towards the corner, no doubt heeding Andy's call. Trevor could see that Kendra would be struggling for cover, and so picked a spot where the Mercedes could be seen and where it would encourage the Land Rover to park close to it, in a row in front of other parked cars. Kendra quickly slid under a white Audi Q5 and waited. She could see the Mercedes with its engine running less than ten feet away and prayed that the owner of the Audi she was hiding under was parked here for the day.

Thank God for SUVs, she thought, as she squirmed into a comfortable position.

It wasn't long before the blue Land Rover arrived, parking next to Trevor, facing the rear of the Mercedes and two cars farther down from where Kendra lay in wait. It would mean squeezing under two more cars to get close to the Discovery, and both were lower than the Audi. The driver, a man in his forties, lowered his window and looked at Trevor, who lowered his.

'I see you got here early, too,' Trevor said with a smirk. 'I guess you've done this before, eh?'

'It seems that you have, too,' the driver said, looking around suspiciously.

'You don't need to worry, mate, this is as good a place as any to do this. No cameras this end, and hardly any foot traffic. We're just a couple of mates meeting up if anyone walks by, that's all.' Trevor grinned.

'What's your name, fella?' the driver asked.

'You don't need to know my name and I don't need to know yours. I just want to see the merchandise so that we can do some business and I'll be on my way,' Trevor said.

'Fair enough, let's get to it, then,' the man said, opening his door.

Both men got out and walked towards the rear of the Discovery. Before opening the boot, they both took one last look around. The passenger, an older man in his fifties, opened the rear door to reveal a large black holdall within. He reached in and unzipped the bag, pulling it open for Trevor to look inside. There, nestled on a bright blue towel, were two new SA80 A3 assault rifles, their durable camouflage coating and streamlined foregrip improvements on those of its predecessor and making it easier to handle. The magazines had been removed and put to one side, and Trevor could see they were both loaded.

'May I?' he asked, his hands open, palms up.

'Yes, but no magazine... yet,' the passenger said.

Trevor looked around to make sure the coast was clear before reaching for one of the rifles. He had previously handled the SA80 A2 and noticed this version was slightly lighter and more comfortable to use. He held it by the foregrip and gave the weapon a good look, checking its features carefully, handling it as someone familiar with weapons would.

Kendra could hear the conversation and could see their legs from her vantage point under the Audi. She guessed that she'd have just a few minutes to get to the Discovery and attach the GPS tag, so she rolled slowly from under the car and straight under the lower Ford Mondeo next to it. It was a tight squeeze and she struggled, but managed to shuffle over to the other side, rolled over again, and slid under a slightly higher Volvo. She shuffled slowly towards the front of it, which faced the nose of the Land Rover. When she reached the engine bay, she had to squeeze her way around it slightly, edging towards the wheels to find more room. She could see the front of the Discovery clearly now and it was within reach. She took the GPS tag from her pocket and removed the tape from the side the adhesive was on. Placing the small, thin tag on the underside of one of the bumpers, she pushed hard to ensure it was fixed well. When she was happy it was secure, she shuffled back towards the rear of the Volvo and waited.

At the Discovery, Trevor was nodding as he cradled the

rifle, taking his time to ensure Kendra had been able to do her thing. Eventually, he looked at the two men and nodded appreciatively.

'This, my friends, is a lovely bit of kit. How much are you asking, again?' he asked, admiring the rifle one last time before placing it back in the holdall.

'It depends on how many you want, fella,' the driver said, 'you can't get these anywhere else but from us. If you want less than five, then it'll be three grand a piece. If you want more than that, then we'll knock off five hundred quid each.'

'That's a lot of money for a rifle, mate, these cost much less than that to buy new,' Trevor argued, knowing that the British Government had paid just over a thousand pounds apiece.

'Yeah, but like I said, where else can you get these? The answer is... nowhere else, so there's a premium on them.'

'I'll tell you what. I'll take twenty of them for two grand each, that's all I'm willing to pay,' Trevor countered.

'You got the money with you?' the passenger asked.

Trevor laughed.

'No, mate, just like you haven't got the twenty rifles with you. Tell me where to bring the money and when I see them all, you'll get it, don't worry. Just make it somewhere sensible, yeah?'

The two men exchanged a look, then nodded.

'How will we reach you?' asked the passenger.

'Same way as before, guys, same way as before. I'll be waiting on your message, see ya,' Trevor said.

After shaking hands, Trevor got into the Mercedes and drove off, leaving the gun runners to reverse out of their parking spot and head for the exit. Only when they were out of Kendra's earshot did she risk coming out from her hiding place. She looked at her filthy hands and clothes and realised she'd have to navigate past a lot of people before she could get to her car.

This should be fun, she thought, as she walked towards the stairwell and a toilet sign that she'd seen earlier.

8

SURVEILLANCE

'*Contact, contact, contact, blue Land Rover Discovery index Romeo-Mike-seven-zero-tango-tango-Juliet now on the exit ramp towards the mini roundabout, two-five over,*' announced the surveillance operative that spotted the Land Rover leaving. '*I can give a direction at the roundabout, if someone can stay behind and pick me up.*'

'I'll pick you up, two-five,' Mike said from his nearby vantage point.

'It's a right, right, right at the roundabout and a loss of vision to two-five,' the operative said.

'*Contact to six-three, continues along Bluewater parkway towards another mini-roundabout and straight over,*' the mobile surveillance unit continued.

Mike Romain called Trevor.

'Okay, mate, we have the vehicle, leave it to us,' he told his old friend.

'Have fun, Mike, just don't get shot, those SA80s in the back are the brand new A3 version, and there's two of them in the boot with full magazines.'

'Received and understood. I'll call later when we house them,' Mike said, and hung up.

Trevor grinned at the thought of working with his old colleague again.

If he can't get it done, then nobody can, he thought, as he drove back towards the factory.

'How's it all going, Mo?' Trevor asked, over the phone.

'We're getting there. The entrances have all been reinforced and we've laid on some extra surprises for them. Amir came up with a cracking idea for the boiler room which he's sorting out now,' Mo replied.

'Good. Just make sure everyone is fully kitted up, okay? The pepper spray is more concentrated when it isn't mixed in with other fluid, so be careful. Also, they'll be bringing more guns next time, so the protective vests are a must.'

'Don't worry, it's all under control. I'm making sure there's nobody on the ground floor this time, or even on the first floor, which will confuse them a little. Our exit strategy is also in place from the third- and fourth-floor windows, which are about thirty to forty feet up. Nobody can climb up, but we'll be able to climb down,' Mo said.

'Once you're outside, do you have everything in place to hold them in?' Trevor asked.

'Yes, Darren has taken care of that, the kit is well hidden near the exits.'

'Great, good job, Mo. I'll head on over to you soon, but I want to stop by the factory first and check in with Andy.'

'Will do, but there's no rush, it's all in hand here and we'll have plenty of warning when they set off to finish up here.'

'Okay, I'll see you later, then,' Trevor said.

He called Kendra.

'How are you doing, love? Everything go to plan?'

'Yes, Dad, the tag is in place, and I've let Andy know so he can keep an eye in case Mike's team struggle. I got filthy so I had to stop and clean up, but I'll be on my way shortly. I'll need to stop off home for a change of clothes, so shall I meet you at the hotel later?'

'Yes, see you there. Mike is keeping a loose follow and talking to Andy. The plan is, when the bad guys eventually stop, the surveillance team won't be spotted and can come in on foot quickly.'

'Great, that's one job out of the way, now we need to get as many of those bastards off the streets when they hit the hotel again,' she said.

'It'll be tougher this time, love, so make sure you have all your kit. I'll call Rick and let him know to be ready.'

'It sounds like you have everything under control,' Rick said when Trevor had updated him.

'We're expecting them to come mob-handed to the hotel next time, so will your lot be able to handle them once we have them contained?'

'Yes. We received an *anonymous* tip that there will be an armed assault somewhere in the docklands area, but nothing more specific. As such, we have people briefed and ready to go at a moment's notice. Another *nine-nine-nine* call will go in that will identify the hotel and how many armed men will be in attendance, which is when our units will be deployed, including the armed response teams and dog handlers. Anything else you need?' Rick asked.

'No. I'll be in touch as soon as we know what's going on,' Trevor replied.

'Great stuff; cheers, Trevor.'

Trevor nodded, happy that the plan was taking shape and that they were as prepared as they could be. He couldn't understand what the uneasy feeling was, until he remembered a number of occasions when things had gone horribly wrong.

Let's hope today isn't one of those days.

ANDY WAS on the phone when Trevor walked into the operations room back at the factory, less than half an hour after leaving Bluewater. He acknowledged him with a wave as he continued his conversation, making a note before ending the call.

'That was Mike Romain. They're just approaching Maidstone so they're keeping back, as it isn't as busy with traffic. I'm giving him updates from the GPS tag so they're aware of exactly where the Discovery is.'

'That's interesting; from what I recall, isn't Maidstone where the missing armourer was originally from?' Trevor asked, recalling the dossier on the weapons thief, Colour Sergeant Reg Malone.

'His parents lived there, yes, but he lives... or is supposed to live somewhere in Plymouth, isn't he?'

'Which is close to the base, so nobody would really think of checking Maidstone, especially since his parents are both dead,' Trevor said. 'He must either know someone there or has gone back there as it is familiar to him, and he thinks he can evade the police.'

'Oh, hang on, the vehicle is turning off, I need to call Mike.'

'MIKE, the vehicle has turned left, left into Sutton Road towards the industrial estate there. Stand by,' Andy said.

'Thanks, Andy, I'll just let the team know quickly.'

'Mike, it's now into Bircholt Road and the Parkwood Industrial Estate. The vehicle is slowing, it's now into a small car park a couple of hundred yards down, and a stop. Tell your units to beware, it's a very small car park,' Andy said.

'Thanks, Andy, leave the rest to us, mate,' Mike said, and relayed the information.

'Seven-three deployed,' came a reply just a few seconds later.

'All received, over to you, seven-three. Units to cover the junctions at Cuxton Road and at Sutton Road,' Mike continued. 'Seven-three, over to you, please confirm when you have vision,' Mike said.

'That's a contact, contact with the vehicle to seven-three. The vehicle is parked at the storage facility opposite the car dealership. I have eyeball on the vehicle and can give an off-off when it moves, but not on the occupants. Nine-two, can you assist?'

'Yes, yes. Nine-two has a contact, contact on two males, both wearing dark clothing, one male taller than the other. The taller male is carrying a large holdall towards the side entrance of the storage facility towards some open shutters. Stand by.'

There was a pause that seemed to last for an age.

'From nine-two, it's unit one-five-zero, unit one-five-zero on the

first floor,' came the almost breathless transmission from the footie, *'and now a loss of vision to me. Seven-three, over to you.'*

'Received by seven-three.'

Mike acknowledged the team members.

'Thank you, seven-three. Great job, nine-two, that couldn't have been easy. Get back to your vehicle, Lynn. You are pretty much done for today, I think.'

'Thanks, boss. Nine-two, out,' Lynn replied. As she had identified the storage unit, Mike now wanted her out of sight in case either of the two men had spotted her.

'The rest of you, hold your position for the off, we'll continue to stay back and work with the GPS location. The next step is to house these bastards. Seven-three, back to you,' Mike said.

THE TWO MEN returned to the Discovery ten minutes later, which remained stationary for two minutes before moving off.

Mike called Andy to let him know.

'We're on a return route, so we'll follow loosely and wait for you to let us know of any deviation. Did you get my message about the storage unit?'

'Yes, thanks, Mike; great job by the team, there. It looks like we've found the guns. I'll be in touch,' Andy said, before turning back to Trevor.

'You may as well go back to the hotel, I'll let you know where they end up.'

'Thanks, Andy. That is a great result about the storage unit. I'll inform the admiral and let him deal with it. Keep an eye out for any movement by the gangs, okay?'

'Don't worry, I can do more than one thing at a time,' Andy said, grinning as he waved Trevor off. 'It would be nice if I could leave this room, though.'

'You'll get your chance, don't you fret. You're too valuable in here and there's nobody else who can do this, so for now, you'll just have to keep that seat nice and warm,' Trevor said.

I should get myself an apprentice, or something, Andy thought as he looked back at the monitors.

9

MAIDSTONE

'How's it going, Mike?' Trevor asked, as he drove back towards the hotel.

'Hi, Trev, I was about to call you. We've just stopped at a Waitrose supermarket in Maidstone, a twenty-minute drive from the storage unit. The footies are out and have followed the two men to the café inside, where they met another man. What did you say this ex-armourer looked like?'

'His name is Reg Malone and he's forty years old, five feet nine, and stocky build,' Trevor replied.

'Yeah, sounds like him. Short light brown hair?'

'Yep. You saying he's in the café there? What's the plan?'

'Well, I'm guessing the two men from the storage unit are the middlemen he's using to sell the guns and he's being cagey even with them. We'll stay on Reg Malone when they split, unless you want us to stay on the Discovery?'

'No, please go with Reg. We have the tag on the Land Rover so we should be able to find them later,' Trevor said.

'Just to be clear, once we've housed Reg, then that's us done, right?'

'On this job, yes, but we'll need your team for the other target in west London, the Vietnamese guy.'

'No problem, I'll let you know when this is all done and dusted and we can discuss the other target later,' Mike said.

'Okay, mate, thanks again for this; great job so far, please thank your team.'

'You can thank them yourself when you give them their little bonus!' Mike laughed.

Trevor grinned as he made his next call.

'Tell me you have good news, Trevor,' Sir Robert said.

'It's partially good news, sir. We've located where we believe the guns are being stored and are now watching Reg Malone so we can house him. He's used a couple of heavies as middlemen so we should also be able to track them later as we have a GPS tag on their vehicle.'

'That's great news, and speedily done, too. Once you've housed Malone, call me immediately so we can split our teams and take the guns and him down simultaneously.'

'Will do, sir. I'll message you the location of the guns so you can start prepping.'

'Good man, Trevor, thank you. Speak soon,' the admiral said.

Trevor's phone rang immediately; it was Kendra.

'I'm parking up now, Dad, same as before. Where do you want to meet?'

'Let's meet at the hotel; we have time, and we'll have notice if they're on the way. Just keep an eye out for any passers-by, I'd rather nobody see us go in.'

A few minutes later they rendezvoused at the hotel entrance. Zoe opened up and let them in.

'The ground and first floors are both secure and ready,' she said. 'Mo is downstairs in the boiler room with Amir and Charmaine.'

They went downstairs and joined the trio as they were overseeing Amir's plan. There was one hose pipe leading from the thermal water heater and another from the steam boiler, both attached and secured with heavy-duty duct tape and zip ties. About six feet from the hose attached to the steam boiler, they saw one of the paint spray guns connected, with one end of the pipe going into the gun and another leaving it. Kendra looked at Amir quizzically.

'I know, it looks rough, but hear me out,' he said. 'The steam will go into the gun, where we have added plenty of pepper spray, which we can keep topping up. It'll mix with the steam and come out the other end as steam on steroids.'

'Will that work?' Trevor asked. 'Won't the steam affect the pepper spray, dilute it in any way?'

'It shouldn't do, it's basically an industrial version of what the police use, but much, *much* hotter and nastier!' Amir laughed.

'Ooh, you evil twin, you,' Kendra said. 'That is likely to sting a lot, isn't it?'

'I truly hope so. Those guys are coming to kill us, remember? The least we can do is blind them and scold them a little. They won't die, but they're likely to be incapacitated for a while. Isn't that what you wanted?'

'Absolutely, Amir, good on you,' Trevor said. 'Although it may be tricky when the police arrive and try to figure out what's happened.'

'Don't worry about that, either,' said Amir. 'Everyone is now wearing gloves, and we've been wiping every surface to make sure they won't find fingerprints. Andy will sort the

CCTV out so that we're never seen, just the baddies getting their arses kicked.'

'I hope they don't start looking into it too much,' Kendra said. 'It's great they won't be able to trace us, but won't they ask a lot of questions?'

'Who will they ask?' Trevor said, 'there won't be anyone here.'

'I know, Dad, but when they see all this and they find out what's happened to the gangsters, as much as they'll enjoy taking them into custody, they will all be asking who the hell did this!'

'I'm guessing that is always going to be a risk we have to take,' Trevor said. 'But as long as we cover our backsides at every scene, then they won't be able to trace anything back to us.'

'Hopefully Rick can also help with that,' Kendra added, thinking ahead.

'Okay, so what about this other hose pipe?' Trevor asked, turning back to Amir.

'That's the thermal water heater, so it'll pump out hot water when we need it.'

'And where do these both lead to?' Kendra asked.

'The steam and pepper spray leads to reception, where the spray can't harm any of us, even with our kit on—I didn't want to take a chance,' Amir replied. 'The hot water leads to the third floor, where it will help with our exit and also with any cleaning that we may need for ourselves, knowing the traps we've set for them. There's some very colourful goo waiting for them!'

'Great,' said Charmaine. 'I doubt they have any idea about what happened to their comrades, so the old traps should still be good with the new arrivals.'

'And everyone will be on the third or fourth floor during the attack?' asked Kendra.

'Yes, all fully kitted and replenished,' Charmaine said. 'Everyone is raring to go.'

'Okay, I guess we can leave you to it, then,' Trevor said, looking around to see if there was anything else to ask about.

'We'll be in constant contact with you all, so don't worry about us,' Mo said, confidently.

'We won't be far away, and as soon as the arseholes are inside, we'll call Rick to get the locals down here. They won't find it easy getting out, and by the time they manage it, they'll be surrounded, all being well,' Trevor said.

'I'm going to go and check upstairs again and make sure everyone is ready,' Charmaine said.

'Any problems, just call,' Kendra told Mo as they all left the room.

'We'll be fine, just make sure you can cart us all out of here,' said Amir.

'We've got the van and one car parked up the road, and another two cars where you left them previously, more than enough for everyone,' Kendra said.

'Nice, you can all take us through the drive-in for a burger on the way back to the factory!'

'Bro, will you stop thinking about your stomach, already!' Mo laughed.

'CONTACT, *contact to five-five, male leaving supermarket via main entrance and towards car park. Loss of vision, seven-three over to you,*' came the call from the footie inside who'd been keeping an eye on Reg Malone.

Once the two middlemen had left in the Land Rover, the surveillance team prepared for Malone to leave quickly, which he did, five minutes later.

The team assembled in an orderly fashion behind and continued to follow the vehicle, before they eventually left Maidstone. Mike decided to call Trevor and update him.

'We're on the move, mate, behind Reg Malone and leaving Maidstone. I'll give you a shout when we house him.'

'That's great, thanks Mike,' Trevor said.

He turned to Kendra. 'It's looking like we're going to be able to take care of the guns issue, knowing how good Mike and his team are. Once the admiral knows the address, he'll deploy his best teams and take the thief and the guns into custody in short shrift.'

'That's good to know,' said Kendra, 'then we can move onto the Vietnamese boss and stop this whole business from getting out of control.'

'I'll call Andy and keep him in the loop,' Trevor said, dialling the number.

'Glad you called, Trev, I have a bit of an update for you,' Andy said.

'What's that, then?' Trevor asked.

'The Land Rover just came to a stop at an address in Chatham, Robin Hood Lane. I'll message the address for your old sea boss.'

'Great, thanks for that. The surveillance team are behind Reg Malone as we speak, so we should be able to house him soon, too,' Trevor said.

'There's something else,' Andy continued, 'I thought I'd do some background checks on the type of extortion that the Vietnamese gang have been carrying out on the hotel owner. You'll like this; not a lot, but it'll tickle your fancy.'

'Get on with it, man, there's a lot going on here and we don't have much time,' Trevor said, somewhat irked.

'The loan shark situation is something that has been springing up regularly all over the country. It's been on a very small scale until recently. I asked Rick to check the police databases and found at least two incidents in each of the major cities, and three more in London, where properties have been handed over to the loan sharks after borrowers failing to pay the extortionate fees. And these are just the ones that have been reported, so there are likely to be many more. These guys are clever, using local muscle to do their dirty work, which is why it isn't showing up as so obvious to the police, because it's never been done like this before. They're rewarding the gangs well, not just for the muscle but also for recruiting potential clients they can extort, it's as if they're working on a commission. And it's successful; they're expanding rapidly. The gangs are making more money doing this than their usual crap; ironically, robberies and burglaries are slightly down, as well as drug seizures.'

'Wow, that's a big operation, and it all leads to this one guy?' Kendra asked.

'Yes, the son of the American gangster is now the big boss here. He's quietly built an empire which is now expanding at an alarming rate, suggesting he is confident of ongoing success. My guess is that he'll be sacrificing his gang allies if anything goes wrong, there'll be plenty more to take over if he needs them.'

'All the more reason to put the bastard out of business quickly,' Trevor said.

'It's not going to be easy getting evidence if he's using the gangs, is it?' Kendra asked.

'Who said anything about getting evidence? We're not the

police, love, remember? As long as we know for sure that he's doing what we think he is, then he's fair game for us. The police can take care of the lowlifes he's using, we'll sort him out in our own way.'

'That's what I love about working with this team,' Andy said, 'we get things done... properly.'

'There's lots to do, so let's get on with it, shall we?' Trevor said. 'Andy, can you figure out a way to get more information on this guy and his organisation?'

'It won't be easy,' he said, 'we need to find out what he's doing and where we can infiltrate his systems.'

'We know he's using a building near the hotel, which the gangs are using, so when we've put this part of the operation to bed we can head on that way and see what we can do,' Trevor replied.

'Okay, in the meantime, I'll gather all the intel I can on their activities around the country.'

'We'll get there, Dad, don't you worry,' Kendra said once Andy had ended the call. Trevor frowned, deep in thought.

'It's true, you know, nobody has ever managed to bring opposing gangs together like this. That man must be looking after them very well indeed, which means they'll fight tooth and nail to protect what they have.'

'Which means it's going to be tough for us, right? Don't forget, Dad, we give as good as we get, remember?'

'I know, love, but until you're a parent, you won't understand that even if you were wearing an *Iron Man* suit, I'd still be worried that you could get hurt!' Trevor smiled as he turned to her. 'And it's not a bad thing, is it? It helps keep me on my toes and gives me extra ideas about how to fight these bastards.'

'I wouldn't have it any other way, Dad,' she replied. 'Now, what's next on the agenda?'

'Let's update Rick and see what mischief we can get him to do, eh?'

'As soon as you give me the nod that the gangs are on the move, I'll put in the anonymous call using the burner phone,' Rick explained. 'That means you'll have twenty-five minutes or so to sort out what you're doing before they arrive, and five to ten minutes before we arrive in force. Just make sure everyone in the team is out safely before we arrive, otherwise it could get very messy.'

'No problem. It's getting to that time where they'll probably make a move. Andy will message us both when it happens.'

'Okay, then. In the meantime, I have some real police work to do; you should try it someday, Detective March.' Rick laughed.

'Very funny. It's a good job you're my boss, otherwise I'd be going off sick with stress for bullying, that would be a real good lesson for you, wouldn't it?'

'Ooh, nasty, don't joke about shit like that, please,' he said. 'Seriously, K: you're doing a terrific job. Speak soon!'

Trevor laughed.

'You have a habit of bringing the best out in people, love. He clearly thinks a lot of you, you know that, don't you?'

'Yeah. He's great, and I'm overjoyed he's on our side,' Kendra said.

Trevor's phone rang.

'Hi, Mike, how's it going?'

'We've housed Reg Malone.'

10

COUNTERATTACK!

The surveillance team eventually followed the vehicle to its destination.

Mike updated Trevor.

'Okay, we've taken him to a holiday home park off Well Street in East Malling. It's called West Well Park, and it's basically a bunch of those luxury static caravans. I've got a footie out as we speak and will get you the number as soon as it's transmitted,' he told Trevor.

'Standby, standby, it's a contact to three-five. The vehicle is parked and unattended outside number seventeen. Three-five, over.'

'Did you get that?' Mike asked.

'Yes,' said Trevor, 'all received, with thanks. Don't hang about there too long, Mike, just give it half an hour or so and then leave it.'

'Will do, thanks. I'll call with a full debrief later and we can discuss the other op,' Mike said. 'Chat later.'

Mike ended the call and transmitted to his team.

'All units, cover the junctions for now, we'll stay here for thirty

minutes and only continue if the subject leaves during that time. Three-five, good job, please return to your vehicle.'

After all the units had acknowledged, Mike made notes that he knew would be seen only by Trevor and his team and sat back, waiting for the operation to conclude. It had been a long but successful day for the surveillance team.

Roll on tomorrow, he thought.

'THAT EXPLAINS why nobody has been able to track him down,' Admiral Jenkins told Trevor on their call, 'pretty clever of the bastard, using a temporary address that he probably paid cash for, and a burner phone, easy to drop off the radar.'

'Yeah, he's pretty switched on,' said Trevor. 'He's probably looking to do another runner once the guns are sold, so you need to do your thing and take him down pretty soon.'

'Oh, don't worry about that, my team are already briefed and just waiting for the address. Now that we have it, they can better plan, and if it's in a holiday park like you said, then they'll have to be extra creative if they want to take him out covertly and without the local constabulary getting involved.'

'I'm sure your highly trained ninjas have done things like this many times!' Trevor laughed.

'They'll be fine, I'm sure. We're splitting the teams so we can retrieve the guns along with the two heavies, I'm keen to ask them some questions about to whom any missing guns have been sold,' the admiral continued.

'You have all three addresses, Admiral, and plenty of skilled manpower, so I'm gonna say that if you can't do it, then nobody can!'

'Good man, Trevor. I appreciate you and your team for doing this, it could have been very embarrassing for the navy. I see no reason why we can't use you for other similar operations. I think we make a good fit, don't you?'

'See, I knew there was a good reason for saving your life all those years ago, you're going to make me rich after all!' Trevor joked.

'You laugh, but I bet after a year or so of some very dodgy jobs, you'll be cursing yourself for ever reconnecting with me!' It was the admiral's turn to laugh. 'Anyway, send me your invoice and we'll take care of it quickly.'

'What would you like me to put down as the services offered, boss?'

'Just make something up, advanced urban training or something official like that.'

'Will do, and thanks again for the opportunity.'

'The pleasure is mine, Trevor, as always. Take care.'

Trevor turned to Kendra.

'I tell you what, he is going to give us a lot of very interesting jobs, if this one is anything to go by.'

'That is a great boost for the business, Dad, we'll be able to put that money to very good use. We can take on a few more trainees and expand the services we offer. The future is looking very bright indeed.'

'In the meantime, let's focus our attention on the current job, there is still a lot to do, daughter.'

ANDY HAD three monitors on the go and his fingers flew across the keyboard as he worked his magic multi-tasking skills to gather as much information as he could for the team, whilst simultaneously watching for movement and anything unusual with the Deptford Mafia and Bethnal Green Boyz. The alerts he'd set up with their known phones as well as the tags placed on the vehicles pinged as movement occurred.

'Here we go,' he said, moving his attention to the trackers on the single monitor. 'That's a lot of phones moving, and it looks like seven, no, eight vehicles. Looks like Trevor was right, they're coming in force this time.'

He called Kendra.

'Hello, Romeo, how art thou?' she asked, giggling when there was no response.

'Stop doing things like that, it's not fair, you know it messes with my head,' he finally said.

'That's why I do it, silly, to toughen you up a little.'

'I'm more than tough, just not when it comes to you. Can I speak freely now, please? I have important news.'

'My apologies, please do go ahead,' Kendra replied, stifling a laugh.

'You have eight vehicles on the way and at least twenty hostiles who I'm sure are very pissed at us, so they'll no doubt be looking for revenge at the hotel. Please let the team know, I'll update you as they get close.'

'Thanks, Andy, I'll call Mo now.'

'Ready the team, Mo, our friends are on the way, at least twenty strong, so make sure everyone is fully kitted and briefed on the exit, okay?'

'Don't worry, Kendra, they know exactly what to do. Just make sure Rick and the cavalry turn up soon after our guests do, so we can get the hell out of here in one piece,' Mo replied.

'Don't you worry, he's my next call,' she said, hanging up and immediately dialling Rick.

'They're on the way, Rick, at least twenty strong and eight vehicles. Their ETA is approximately twenty-five minutes. We estimate they'll all be inside the hotel within five minutes of arrival,' she told her sergeant.

'Great. I'll place the call now and the team will roll out within ten minutes, so that will coincide with our arriving ten minutes after them. Make sure the team is safely away when we get there, okay?'

'It's all in hand, don't worry,' Kendra said, 'I'll call if there's any changes.'

'You ready for this, love?' Trevor said, smiling as he moved the car into position, out of sight. Both were now wearing their protective vests under their coats and had their tactical helmets and masks to hand, along with taser guns and other equipment they'd likely need if things became heated.

'Always ready, Dad; I'm well trained, remember? We'll kick the living shit out of them all,' she said, grinning at her father as he shook his head theatrically.

'I've created a monster,' he said.

INSIDE THE HOTEL, the team were calmly going about their business, knowing they had done everything that had been asked of them in preparation for the attack. Darren collected the equipment he'd need for securing the doors, and took Izzy, Jimmy and Martin outside, where he gave them what they'd need to put their plan into action.

'Remember, listen for my call before you do anything, and just stay out of the way until they're all inside.'

'No problem, D. We'll stick around until we're sure the rest of the team are clear before leaving, right?' Izzy said.

'Yes, we don't leave until everyone is accounted for, but don't do anything stupid, because the Old Bill are on the way. Timing is everything, lads, so let's not screw this up.'

'Don't worry, Darren, the team are on the ball. You've seen how good they are, so as long as we focus on our jobs, I'm not worried at all,' Jimmy added.

'Good, now get yourselves into position. The last thing we need is to be spotted before anything happens,' Darren said, patting them each on the back as they left to take up their positions.

'CHECK the ropes one more time, at each of the four windows,' Charmaine told Zoe. She was confident their escape routes were secure but wanted to keep everyone busy as they waited.

'Will do,' Zoe confirmed, and left.

'Amir, are you sure that thing is gonna work?' she asked the twin as he checked the hose was securely taped to the frame of the door leading to the stairwell. He had cut away a section of the frame so that the hose would fit snugly and not be too obvious when the gangsters broke in. By the time anyone noticed it, it would be too late.

'It's secure, yes. I'll be alone downstairs and will wait for the signal that they're inside. Once I turn it on, I'll be making my way upstairs, hopefully before they get into the stairwell,' Amir said.

It was probably the riskiest of the traps they'd put in place, as it was the one most likely to bring a team member into contact with the gangsters until they got to the third floor. Amir was confident and had volunteered to be the one to put himself at risk.

'Nice one, Amir. If it works the way you anticipate, then this should be a breeze,' Charmaine said.

'If it doesn't, you can blame Mo, it's always his fault when something goes wrong.'

'Everyone get into position,' Mo said, 'ETA is less than five minutes.'

They each got into position inside the hotel, most on the third floor, some on the fourth, and Amir on his own in the basement. Within seconds, it was eerily quiet as they waited. Those within sight of other team members grinned confidently, but they were under no illusions: what they were about to deal with was extremely dangerous.

Mo received the first call, from Trevor.

'Mo, you have the vehicles inbound, they'll be with you in about thirty seconds,' he said. 'Remember, we have a small window here, try and get the team out in the next five minutes, whatever happens.'

'Will do,' Mo said, and ended the call. 'ETA thirty seconds, everyone,' he shouted. He called his brother and told him to wait for his signal before turning on the steam hose.

The cars turned up, some with wheels squealing as they came to an overly dramatic halt near the front entrance. From their secure positions, Darren and his three colleagues watched and waited.

Raheem Abdi, the Deptford Mafia boss so embarrassed

on the previous attempt, got out of the passenger seat of his vehicle. He was quickly joined by Imran Aziz, the Bethnal Green Boyz' leader. They both watched as the rest of their combined gangs gathered near the front entrance, waiting for their signals. Many carried baseball bats, some had handguns, and three had rifles. Some of them also had crowbars and pick axes, ready for a tough entry.

Darren had purposely made it more difficult for them to break in this time, hoping it would lure them into a false sense of accomplishment when they got through. He wanted them to work for it, and so had used wooden batons to barricade each of the doors. He figured it would take a few attempts before the batons snapped in two.

'Let's see what the fuss is all about, eh?' Imran said to Raheem, smiling at his former adversary.

'Fabian and Mervin, take one man each and go to the other doors,' Raheem shouted. He turned to Imran, frowning.

'Don't get too cocky, Imran, whoever was in that cursed hotel last time was good enough to take out eight of my men. We weren't prepared last time; this time we are. Let's see how your boys do, eh?'

Imran flashed a smile and turned to the waiting men.

'Okay, boys, let's show what happens to those that decide to take us on,' he shouted, 'now break those damned doors down!'

Three men quickly approached the main doors and started barging, testing them, one of them remembering it had been easier the previous time.

'You two start kicking, and I'll use the crowbar,' he shouted.

His colleagues nodded and proceeded to kick, taking turns to violently attack the door while he tried to jemmy it open. After each kick, he was able to make a tiny amount of progress until eventually the crowbar was in its optimum position.

'Ray, help me with this,' he called to a fourth man, who came and grabbed the crowbar with him. 'When I say, you pull as hard as you can!'

At the next kick, he shouted 'now!' and they levered the crowbar fully towards them, bending the door frame, weakening the locks. They pushed the crowbar back in and waited for the next kick.

'Again!' he shouted. Their efforts were rewarded as the door slammed inwards. The gangsters cheered and surged forward brandishing their weapons, eager to take the fight to whoever was inside.

'Come on, then, what are you waiting for?' Imran said, laughing as he turned away from Raheem and ran towards the door.

'Fool,' Raheem muttered as he ran behind, eager to appear as if he were doing his share.

As they entered the hotel lobby, Imran and Raheem directed their men to cover the entryways, but not to do anything until they were ordered. The lobby was gloomy within until someone found the light switch. Nobody noticed the door that they'd broken through being closed behind them, such was their eagerness to fight, the adrenalin driving them. Nobody was aware that the two rear entrances had also been closed, and that the four men deployed to them had now also joined the crowd in the lobby.

'I told you all, be careful, these bastards are sneaky. Take your time and watch for any traps that will slow you down or even hurt you,' Raheem shouted.

'One floor at a time, boys,' Imran added, 'and watch yourselves, like our friend Raheem just said.'

Before anyone went through the doors to the stairwells, one of the gangsters noticed something odd in the door frame. He could see that the frame had been cut away and what looked like some sort of pipe was now starting to smoke. He moved in for a closer look, but before he could act, the pepper-infused steam reached his eyes and blinded him immediately, causing him to scream in agony. His colleagues started shouting as the steam started to affect them, some crying out in pain, others moving their arms frantically in front of them as they lost their sight. Within seconds, the hotel lobby was a large mess of crying men, some now on the floor, others heading towards the exit in a frantic attempt to escape.

Raheem and Imran were farthest away from the hose and so weren't immediately affected.

'What the hell is happening?' Imran asked, alarmed by the sudden carnage.

'I told you they set traps, didn't I? Damn them! We need to get out, now!' Raheem shouted, running for the exit.

Outside, Darren had placed four wedges under the doors to prevent them from being opened outwards and had also fed a length of heavy chain through the door handles. At the other exits, Izzy, Jimmy and Martin had done the same.

Raheem quickly realised they had been trapped, and turned to face his men, some of whom had not yet been affected.

'Upstairs, quickly! Everyone upstairs, we need to leave this floor!'

They quickly smashed through the doors but were too slow to see the fleeing Amir as he scurried back upstairs, his job well done, and now fully kitted and ready for the next phase.

'Good job, bro,' Mo said as he scampered through the doors to the third floor.

'That was fun, they're all over the place!' Amir grinned. 'We should start getting people out, we don't need everyone to stay.'

'Agreed,' said Mo. 'Go up to the fourth floor and start helping them out, I'll do the same here. You can stay and deal with the other traps, but I want everyone out as soon as possible. We have less than ten minutes, remember?'

Amir ran upstairs and joined Zoe and the team that was guarding the fourth floor.

'Get everyone out,' he told her. 'The police are on the way, and we need to be out of here as soon as possible.'

'Got it,' Zoe said calmly. 'Let's go, everyone, that's the signal for us to get the hell out of here!'

Down one level, Mo was overseeing the exodus through two of the windows selected. Clive and Rory had stayed behind to cover the floor in case the gangsters came up too quickly. The rest were to leave urgently. The window exits selected were not obvious, being in bathrooms, so that it would be difficult for the invading gangs to find them.

The fourth-floor windows were opened, and the ropes were unfurled. Charmaine, Zoe, Danny and Greg left within seconds of each other, shimmying down quickly to the bottom, where they were met by Danny's team and ushered towards the vehicles parked nearby. Clive and Rory joined their colleagues downstairs. Mo and Amir had decided they would stay a little longer to ensure that none of the gang managed to reach them before everyone had made their exit.

The first two gang members avoided the caltrops left for

them on the stairs as they cautiously made their way up. The first two through the doors to the third floor were met with a blast from Mo's spray gun, hitting them square in the face, sending them recoiling backwards down the stairs in agony. Amir had come down a floor and was busy spraying the first man through the doors.

The twins could hear whimpering, along with angry shouting from below both stairwells, and knew they'd have to make their way out. The racket was soon replaced with calm voices, and Amir could only hear the odd word here and there. Concerned that the attackers were about to rush the doors and overpower him, he quickly put a chain through the handles and padlocked the doors shut. Satisfied that it would take several minutes to get through, he made his way to the room, where he knew a rope would be waiting for him. He quickly released the adjoining rope so nobody else could use it, and then manoeuvred himself outside, ready to shimmy down. Before doing so, he slowly closed the window as much as he could in an attempt to hide the rope, before confidently abseiling down to where Darren was waiting.

'Where's Mo?' Darren asked.

'He should be right behind me,' Amir said, looking up nervously, hoping to see his brother. 'Maybe I should go back.'

'No, Amir, I'm sure he'll be fine. Make your way to the cars and I'll wait for him. The police will be here soon.' Darren looked towards the road anxiously.

Amir looked up one last time before heading towards the cars.

'You'd better get your arse out of there as soon as you can, brother,' he muttered as he ran.

Born to Kill

11

CAPTURE

Mo had heard the change in the gang's mood and decided to deal with it slightly differently than his brother. Instead of chaining the doors shut as Amir had done, he simply locked them and made his way to the exit. He made his way into the bathroom and saw that both windows were still open with their respective ropes. It was then that he realised he'd need to leave one of the ropes in place, giving the gang an opportunity to leave.

'Well, that's not gonna happen,' he said with a smirk, as he looked outside and saw what he needed to do. 'Time to use some of my baby brother's parkour skills, that should upset him.'

Working as quickly as he could, he untied the first rope, watching as it fell to the ground below. He could see someone waiting for him down there and made his way to the second rope. Hearing a dull thud, he assumed the gang were trying to breach the doors and paid no more attention to it. He was finally able to untie the second rope and got ready to leave via the drainpipe that was less than six feet away from the window, one that wasn't available for his twin farther along. He was confident that he'd make it and balanced himself on the ledge as he prepared to make the jump.

It was at that moment that a pair of gang members rushed into the bathroom and grabbed him by the legs, pulling him roughly to the floor. He hit his head on the sink as he fell, which stunned him momentarily. Before he could clear his head and respond to the attack, the two men started punching and kicking him as he lay there, trying to cover his head, rolling into a ball.

'Enough!' came an angry shout from a third person entering the room. Raheem looked down at the prone prisoner, tempted to lash out and cause grievous damage to the person who had embarrassed him so much. 'Pick him up,' he shouted.

The two men propped Mo up against the wall and pinned him there, awaiting further instructions. Raheem walked to the window and looked down, seeing someone else on the ground floor, probably waiting for his friend. He turned back to Mo, whose head was now clear enough to recognise that he was in a lot of trouble. The protective vest had dulled most of the blows, but he was still hurting from the punches and kicks to his limbs, along with several to his head.

'Where are my men?' Raheem asked, staring malevolently into Mo's eyes.

'I... I don't know what you're talking about,' Mo lied, trying to think of a cover story that would give him a chance of survival.

'I think you do,' Raheem said, continuing to stare. 'So tell me where they are, or I'll throw you out of the window... now.'

Mo believed him; the man had not flinched when making the threat. His mind whirred, knowing his life was at risk.

'You do that, and you'll never see them again,' Mo finally said, his voice firm and confident.

Raheem smiled and nodded respectfully, not having expected that response.

'Very good. That means we can have some fun with you later, then, doesn't it? I'm sure you will change your mind, we have some fun ways of making people talk!' He laughed, looking to his men, who were also laughing, knowing what their boss was likely to do.

Another man came into the now-overcrowded bathroom.

'Raheem, we found a rope in another room, it looks like they have all escaped!'

'Bring him!' Raheem told his men, who dragged Mo with them as they followed. 'Send some of the boys to check the rest of the floors, in case they're trying to trick us again!'

In the bathroom where Amir had made his escape, Imran waited with one of his Bethnal Green Boyz.

'Not afraid of heights, are you?' he teased Raheem, 'it's only thirty-odd feet.'

'You two go down now and wait for this one, we'll be right behind you,' Raheem said, ignoring the barb.

Imran nodded and pushed his man towards the rope, where he quickly positioned himself to make his way down. Just as he was being lowered, Imran put up a hand and pointed towards the distant road.

'I might be wrong, but that looks like a lot of vehicles coming our way in a hurry, some with blue lights. We need to get the hell out of here, fast!'

DARREN HAD SEEN the stranger looking down at him from the window on the third floor and realised Mo was in big trouble.

'Shit,' he muttered.

He picked up his phone. 'Trev, they've got Mo, what do you want me to do?'

'I was about to call you. Get out of there, now; Rick and the police are almost here!'

'Damn, what about poor Mo?'

'There's nothing we can do for him now. Rick will be here soon, hopefully they can rescue him,' Trevor said, 'now get the hell out of there, Darren!'

Darren hung up and started running towards the parked vehicles, cursing as he did so.

'Amir is not gonna be happy,' he muttered.

'SHIT! GET A MOVE ON, MAN!' Raheem shouted to Imran, who was preparing to follow his man down the rope.

'Leave him and get out now!' Imran shouted.

'No! He's coming with us, he knows where my men are, and I want them back!' Raheem pushed Mo towards the rope. 'Now, go!'

Imran disappeared out of sight and Mo was quickly pushed into position.

Raheem squared up to him. 'My men are waiting down there, you can either go down and live, or I can throw you out now and you can die, your choice.'

'Live,' Mo said, staring back defiantly. Inwardly, he prayed that the team would be able to track and rescue him, soon, before he was hurt—or worse.

He was hoisted up onto the ledge and made his way down to Amir.

Raheem saw the convoy of vehicles was close and realised that using their cars to escape was now impossible.

'Damn them!' he said as he lifted himself to ready for his escape. 'Damn them all!'

THE REST of the team were safely in their vehicles when Rick and the police convoy arrived, so they were able to drive away from the scene without being noticed. The hotel was quickly surrounded by the police team that Rick had chosen for the job. Most of his Serious Crime Unit were present and had been partnered with a Territorial Support Group officer who was specially trained in riot training and entering hostile buildings. The TSG crew had been briefed, and quickly covered the hotel's entrances. As the two gangs were believed to be heavily armed, there were also armed officers, along with several dog units and special search teams. They were well prepared.

'Remember, these bastards won't hesitate to shoot. There's also likely to be hazardous materials inside, according to my source, so be careful,' Rick instructed.

He indicated for the entry teams to ready themselves and gave the signal to proceed. A TSG officer and their SCU partner approached each entrance with heavy bolt croppers. They removed the wedges that were preventing the doors opening outwards and proceeded to cut the chains. When the chains were removed, they gave hand signals, making sure their colleagues were out of harm's way when the doors were opened. At the main entrance, the doors were quickly yanked open to reveal the reception area within.

'Wait for it!' Rick shouted as he took stock of the mess inside. He could see several men lying on the floor, rolled up in a ball, whimpering, but he knew how dangerous these men were and would not risk anyone going inside until he was happy it was safe.

'This is the Metropolitan Police,' he shouted. 'We are an armed unit and will react to any threats that you make. Come out with your hands up and you will be taken safely into custody.'

The response was instant as rapid gunshots came from a machine rifle, firing wildly into the space where the doors had once been, some hitting the gang's cars that were parked in line with the doors. Rick had been correct in his assumption and his warnings had been heeded as the police back-up units had all taken cover to the side where they were safe from the gunfire. He turned to the man on his left, Inspector Paul Jenkins of the MO19 Specialist Firearms Command.

'You owe me a tenner, Guv. I told you they'd respond like that,' said Rick, with a grin.

'You did, but we have to follow procedure, Rick, as much as we don't like it. Anyway, now that we know, we can do our thing, can't we? I love this part.'

He spoke into his radio, which connected him to the rest of his team, one sergeant and eight constables, all highly trained in all aspects of firearms, and all very experienced in entering hostile locations.

'Standby, standby,' he relayed.

At the sound of the second 'standby,' a huge explosion was heard at the rear of the hotel, the opposite aspect to the main entrance, as pre-planned by the unit. The distraction device placed there, a forty-gallon oil drum filled with explosives, was appropriately named; immediate attention was focused on the rear, where the gang members now thought they would be targeted. As the attention shifted from the front, two flash bangs were thrown through the main entrance, setting off two further loud bangs along with smoke, which was released on detonation. The magnesium flares were very effective and many of the gang fell to their knees clutching the side of their heads, stunned into submission.

The sergeant and eight armed officers moved quickly through the doors, their Sig Sauer MCX rifles at the ready, shouting for people to get down. This went on for some time and intermittent shouts came from within as the armed officers searched the building for more threats. After what seemed like an eternity, the sergeant was the first to come back out into the open, bringing one of the gang members with him, now safely zip-tied and groggy from his experience.

'Lie down!' shouted the sergeant, which the young man immediately did, helped by his captor so that he wouldn't fall flat on his face.

Other firearms officers started bringing out more prisoners, who were placed on the ground one at a time. After just a few minutes, sixteen gang members were arrayed neatly in a row. Each one had an evidence bag placed next to him, with property that had been taken from them.

'Ready for the handover, Sergeant?' Inspector Jenkins asked.

'Yes, sir, ready for collection,' replied John Bell, the MO19 sergeant, the job successfully completed.

'Uniform units, over to you, Jane,' Jenkins said to the TSG inspector standing next to him.

'Thanks, Paul, we'll take it from here,' Inspector Jane Finlay replied. She moved towards her colleagues, all similarly kitted in their riot gear, and indicated for them to move towards the prisoners. Two dog units also moved into the hotel to ensure there were no others hiding.

'Sir, you should come and see this,' John Bell told his boss. 'You need to see this, too, Rick.'

They followed him to the row of prisoners, where he pointed to three of them.

'These three had some worrying weapons in their possession when we moved in,' Bell said, opening one of the larger evidence bags.

'Shit,' Rick said, instantly recognising the SA80 rifle that the team had been tracking for the First Sea Lord. He said nothing more, to avoid potentially awkward questions later.

'Where the hell did they get those from?' asked Jenkins. 'That's as good as anything we've got. Luckily for us, they don't know how to use the damned things.'

'I had a close look and the serial numbers have been shaved off, I doubt they'll be traceable now,' said Bell.

'That's a shame, because someone has screwed up massively for these bastards to have these weapons, haven't they?' Jenkins said, shaking his head.

Rick breathed an inward sigh of relief when Bell informed them of the serial numbers. That would mean that the navy would be kept out of it, for now. Then something dawned on him.

'There's only sixteen? I was told there were more than twenty in total; have the dogs cleared the rest of the hotel?' he asked.

'They just completed the sweep, there was nobody else,' said Jenkins.

Jane Finlay approached them.

'My team have found a rope from a third-floor window,' she explained, 'so there's a chance some of them have escaped.'

'Damn it!' said Rick, 'they must have seen us coming, probably had a spotter at the end of the road or something.'

'I'll get some of my team to do a sweep of the area, we may get lucky,' Finlay said, 'I'll get the dog units to assist.'

'Thanks, Guv,' Rick said, 'I'm guessing they're long gone now, but it's worth a try.'

He moved to one side as the prisoners were propped up one by one and taken to the vans that had been called to transport them. He called Trevor.

'Any sign of Mo, Rick?' Trevor asked immediately.

'Sorry, no. We've had dogs go through, and there's no trace of anyone else. There are sixteen prisoners, so some have gotten away,' Rick whispered. 'I'm guessing they're on foot somewhere and probably looking to make their way back to west London.'

'Shit!' Trevor exclaimed, 'how the hell did that happen?'

'We think they used the same rope to get out as the team did,' Rick said. 'Is Amir doing okay?'

'We had to pull him away from the cars when he found out. Kendra, Darren and Charmaine are with him now, trying to calm him down. He wants blood, for sure,' Trevor said.

'I'll have to go, mate, there's a lot to do here. One thing you need to know, they found three SA80 rifles with this lot, with the serial numbers filed away. You need to tell your navy buddies about it, this is bad news. Hopefully there aren't many more out there, but the navy needs to know that some London gangs now have their rifles.'

'Okay, thanks, Rick. Call me with any updates, I'll do the same when we track down where they've taken Mo. I'm hoping he has his GPS tag with him so Andy can find him quickly.'

'Good luck, talk later,' Rick said, ending the call and walking back towards the throng of police officers at the hotel.

'It's gonna be a long night,' he said.

12

WHERE IS MO?

Mo watched as one of the gang members casually broke into the white Ford Transit van that was parked outside a logistics company on a nearby industrial park, one of many similar vehicles parked overnight until the early morning shift. Nobody would notice it missing until then, so it was a safe bet the gang would use it to get back to west London. Having started the vehicle, the rest of what was left of Raheem and Imran's gangs, just five of them in total, jumped in the back, with Imran in the driver's seat and Raheem his passenger.

'Search him,' Raheem ordered, 'make sure he doesn't have a phone or any weapons on him, these bastards are well equipped.'

Mo had anticipated this would happen at some point and had managed to move his small GPS tracker disc from his back pocket to somewhere the gang were unlikely to search —his underpants—before they'd tied his hands behind his back once he'd shimmied down the rope at the hotel. The man searching him removed his mobile phone and turned it off, passing it to Raheem in the front. Raheem knew it could be tracked, so he threw it out as they drove out of the industrial park. They removed some unused zip-ties and a small multi-functional pocket knife his brother had given him, along with some cash he always carried on operations like this. None of the team carried identification, and always used burner phones when away from the factory.

'That's it, Raheem,' the searcher said, 'he won't bother us with anything.'

'Good, because I want some time with him when we get back,' Raheem replied.

'You should call Ray now, you know, give him the heads-up that we've properly screwed up. He isn't gonna be happy, you know,' Imran said, shaking his head nervously.

'There's not a lot we can do about that, is there, Imran? Let's get this piece of shit back and Ray can ask the questions himself.' Knowing Imran was correct, he dialled Raymond Kam's number.

'Tell me that you have the bastard owner, Raheem. Tell me that the hotel is in our possession,' the Vietnamese boss asked calmly.

'Sorry, boss, we've hit some problems. The police turned up in force, hundreds of them. Only a few of us managed to escape,' said Raheem. The silence was deafening as Raheem waited for a reply.

'Boss, before you get angry,' he continued, 'we have a prisoner with us, we're bringing him to you. He'll be able to tell us where my men are and where the hotel owner is, I'm sure.'

'You better hope he does, Raheem,' Kam said, hanging up.

'That sounded like it went well,' Imran said with a grin.

'I'm glad you find this so funny, Imran. Do you not understand what's just happened tonight? Our gangs, *both* gangs, are finished! It's just you and one man left in yours, and two in mine, not much of a gang, are we? You think that's funny?'

Imran's tone changed as he turned to his passenger.

'Best we make this work then, eh? The only chance we have of salvaging anything from this mess is by making sure Ray gets what he wants, because only he can look after us now.' He turned back to the road ahead.

'It's more than that, my friend. We either get him what he wants, or we die, it's as simple as that, eh?' Raheem replied. It was his turn to grin.

'Andy, you're on speaker. They have Mo,' Kendra said, 'and we think they're heading back west. Check his tracker and see if he still has it on him.' Her fingers were firmly crossed that the tracker was in Mo's possession.

'Bloody hell, how did that happen?'

'Never mind that now, focus on finding him so we can get him back before anything happens.'

'On it, stand by,' Andy said, reverting to professional mode as he brought up the tracker program. He input the team tracker codes and waited a second before the screen came to life.

'Okay, I have the team in two groups heading towards the factory, and I have one tag heading in the opposite way at speed. It's Mo's signal, as expected, and they must be in a vehicle, now on the A406 North Circular Road heading west.'

'Damn, they got mobile quick,' Kendra said. 'How do you want to do this, Dad?'

'Andy, prep your van; we'll need the drones and some

entry kit. We'll be with you in about ten minutes so be ready to move out. We need to move tonight, otherwise I fear for Mo.'

'Received and understood, Marge will be ready when you arrive,' said Andy.

As soon as the call ended, Andy went to the car park at the rear of the factory where his beloved camper van was parked. Heavily modified, it was now a state-of-the-art operations vehicle that allowed the team to function on the move and therefore more efficiently. He quickly started the engine to warm her up and then plugged in the two drones he was likely to use when they arrived at their destination, affectionately named Mabel and Tim. Both had been very effective in past operations, with Tim small enough to fly silently indoors without detection. Once happy that everything was on charge, he switched on the numerous computers and monitors that were set up in the back, readying the tracker program.

'Hang in there, Mo,' he whispered, watching his friend move quickly towards North Acton and the clutches of the Vietnamese.

'MARK, sorry to disturb you so soon, but we have a situation and may need some assistance,' Trevor told the surveillance chief.

'We're prepped and ready to go early tomorrow as it is, Trev, what's going on?' Mike Romain replied.

'One of our men has been taken by the gangs. We believe they're heading towards the plot you'll be setting up on tomorrow morning. We're just heading back to the factory to get some kit and then we'll be on our way over there. Can you get there sooner than originally planned in case the situation develops? We're planning to tag vehicles when we get there, which should help you on any follows tomorrow onwards,' Trevor said.

'Sure,' said Mike, 'I'll call the team and get them there first thing. In the meantime, I'll drive down tonight and join you; Clara is away for the week so I'm alone and bored.'

'Happy for you to join us. We'll see you there in an hour or so, thanks again,' said Trevor.

Minutes later, the team arrived at the factory. They quickly disembarked from their vehicles and went about their business with an efficiency that made Kendra proud, seeing them act so professionally when one of their own was in such extreme danger. She looked for Amir and found him in the equipment locker, loading an extra taser gun and kit into a second backpack. He turned to Kendra as she walked in.

'It's for Mo, for when we get him back,' he said calmly as he continued to load the kit.

'You sure you're okay, Amir? Shouldn't you stay here while we go and get him?' She knew full well what the answer was going to be.

'Are you kidding? If I'm not there to help rescue my own brother, I'll never be able to forgive myself,' he said, his voice choking as he stood there, shaking. Kendra gave him a hug.

'I know I joke about him and call him names, but he's my twin brother, Kendra, and I don't know what my life would be like without him in it.' Amir released himself from the embrace.

'I understand, love, of course you should be there. And I'll be standing right next to you, making sure you take the mickey out of him when he's safely back with us.'

'Oh, I'll be taking the piss out of him, don't you worry, but before that, I may have to give him a dig in the ribs for scaring me like this.'

'You mean like the time you did it to him?' she said, reminding Amir that he had put himself in danger far more frequently than his older twin.

'Fair enough, but I'm still gonna do it,' he said, smiling finally as he secured the two backpacks.

'Yep, I guessed as much,' Kendra said, rolling her eyes. 'Now, let's go and get him back, eh?'

THE TEAM WERE FULLY KITTED and had time to take on some refreshments before leaving in a convoy which quickly split as they reached the main roads. Marge, driven by Kendra, was at the rear of the convoy, with Trevor, Amir and Andy in the back, keeping an eye on Mo's GPS tag.

'Looks like they're approaching the Hanger Lane gyratory,' Andy said, 'which means they're only a couple of minutes away from where we think they're going to go.'

'So, we're almost an hour behind, right?' Amir asked.

'Maybe less, depends on traffic,' said Trevor. 'Andy, what else can you tell us about this industrial estate where they seem to congregate?'

'The two gangs are staying in the Travelodge there, but I'm not so sure about the Vietnamese elements. Hopefully we'll find out more when it's confirmed where they're about to go to,' Andy replied.

'What about the Vietnamese, did you find anything else?' Kendra asked.

'A little. As I told you before, their operation is far-reaching and has impacted many of our cities. They've focused on taking over commercial premises such as hotels and businesses in the main, and some domestic housing. Interestingly, they have used the same company name to register their business interests and one of them is near that Travelodge. There's a small row of three shops, with four flats above them over two storeys, sandwiched between a pub that's being converted and some new office buildings. That entire block is registered to Raymond Kam's company, Legacy Solutions. I looked on the map and there's a road to the rear that allows access to the flats.'

'Okay, where exactly is that?' Trevor asked.

'It's Victoria Road, which looks like it goes around in a loop. It's almost opposite the holiday Inn, there.'

'That looks like a tough place to cover, Mike's team is likely to struggle to get close in,' Trevor mused.

'If we can get someone down that access road to add a couple of cameras, then we should be fine, and we won't need to get in too tight. I agree, they'll stick out like a sore thumb there,' Andy said.

'Leave that to me,' Amir said confidently, 'I can do that.'

'Thanks, Amir. Before we do anything, though, I'm inclined to send up one of the drones to have a look, make sure there's nothing that can cause us problems. For all we know, they may have their own surprises,' Andy said.

'Is that them arriving now?' Kendra asked, pointing to the signal that had slowed, and was now turning into the access road.

'Yep.'

'I'll call the team and let them know to hang back for now, we need to plan this carefully,' Trevor said, taking out his phone.

'It looks like they've moved Mo into one of the flats, to the far left of the block as you look from the front where the shops are. Unfortunately, I can't tell which flat, so we need to find out for ourselves,' Andy said. 'Amir, I'll ready a few of the micro cameras, make sure you have them cover all possible entrances and windows, so we have an idea of movement.'

Amir nodded. 'Understood.'

'Once we've narrowed it down, I can try and get in close with Tim,' Andy added, referring to the thumb-sized, silent drone used so effectively in the past. 'It's important we know exactly where he's being held before we can try and rescue him.'

'We have no idea how many goons this Kam guy has with him, do we?' Kendra asked.

'No, so we shouldn't take any chances. Interestingly, they've put this address down as Legacy Solutions' registered company address, which means this is where his business documents and computers are located, and where they direct their nationwide campaigns from. If that's the case, I need access to it so we can do some real damage,' Andy said.

'Any idea how we can do that?' Kendra asked.

'As this is the registered address, it stands to reason that all legal correspondence is sent here, which means we can email an infected file. We just need an email address,' Andy said, 'which isn't as easy as you think. These guys don't have a regular website or social media presence where you can just message them easily.'

'Why don't we ask Mr Khan if they've sent him anything by email? My guess is they try and look legitimate by sending something official, so they have a cover story if anything is investigated,' Trevor said. 'Let me call and find out.'

As Trevor made his call, Andy indicated to Mo's GPS signal and said, 'it's moving back and forth within a small area, suggesting he's been left in a small room. That's a good sign that they've just left him alone for now,' Andy said, nodding at Amir.

'Knowing my brother, he'll be plotting two things: one, how to escape; and two, if he can't escape, to fight like a lunatic and make them pay for what they're about to do to him.'

'We may be able to get to him before that,' Kendra said. 'Let's not focus on the negative just yet.'

'They've left him for a reason, maybe the person they brought him to isn't here yet,' Andy added.

'If you give me a handful of GPS tags I'll stick them on any cars I find,' said Amir.

'Good idea,' Kendra said. 'Let's cover all eventualities.'

RAHEEM TOLD one of his men to take the van and dump it a few miles away, preferably in a car park somewhere well away from Kam's building. They dragged Mo to a doorway at the rear of a hair salon, the middle of the three shops, which led to a stairwell. The went to the second floor and the flat above the fried chicken takeaway, where they locked Mo in a small, empty, windowless room, just nine feet by six.

Mo searched every inch of the room for something to help him escape but found nothing. He stopped and listened for voices... again, nothing. He paced the room, considering his options, wondering what was likely to happen to him, and whether the team were close by. He felt for the GPS tag that was still neatly tucked in his underpants, praying that it still functioned, thinking of one thing and one thing only.

Where are you, brother?

'WE HAVE good news and potentially bad news,' Trevor said, having ended his call with hotelier Kamal Khan.

'Go on,' Kendra said.

'Mr Khan did indeed receive several emails, before he had any contact in person with Raymond Kam. It was to do with a legitimate offer to buy the hotel at a price that I imagine was well below market value, to take the debt into account. There's no mention of any debt or loan as it would have implicated Kam, so it was clever to make that offer in advance of any potential investigation.'

'That's great, so what's the bad news?' Andy asked.

'It isn't from a personal email address, but a Legacy Solutions standard company email: admin at legacysolutions dot com,' Trevor replied.

'Why is that bad?' Kendra asked.

'Don't we need Kam himself to open the email? What if we send something and it goes to one of his minions?' queried Trevor.

'That doesn't matter,' Andy said, 'in fact, I'm hoping it does get opened by one of his staff; as long as someone opens it, we'll be in.'

'How do we make them open an email?' Kendra asked, 'won't they have spyware programs or something?'

'Nothing that can detect my trojan viruses, no. And I'll send an email from an official body, which they will definitely want to open, especially as it will dispute ownership of the Liverpool hotel they recently acquired.'

'How?' Amir asked.

'I'm going to send them a default notice from Land Registry, who record all property and land purchases. I'll say the purchase has been disputed and that it will be investigated unless evidence of the purchase is sent along with contact information of their solicitor.'

'I suppose that would do it, yes,' Amir replied. 'You are one devious cop, you know that?'

'Ex-cop, Amir; they threw me out, remember?'

'Once a cop, always a cop, Andy. Don't try and pull the wool over my eyes, mate; I may be young, but I see things and I notice things.'

'I'll attest to that,' Kendra said, 'there is much more to our Amir here than meets the eye.'

'And best of all, he's on our side,' Trevor added.

'Right, now we've cleared that up, how are you going to do this, Amir?' Andy handed him a small bag containing the cameras and GPS tags.

'Once you've given the all-clear with a flyover, then I'll simply walk in and do my thing.' Amir winked.

'Best you help me with Mabel, then, eh?' Andy said.

'Mabel, Marge, Tim, is there any kit you haven't named?' Trevor asked.

'Everything has a name, Trev, you should know that by now.'

'Let's get cracking, shall we?' Kendra said, 'we have a friend to rescue.'

13

RECOVERY

'How's it going, gang?' Mike asked as he joined them in the rear of the camper van.

'As good as it can be, I suppose,' said Trevor. 'Andy's just flying over the target area now so we can check for any surprises. So far, there's nothing that concerns us too much.'

'I wouldn't speak too soon if I were you,' Andy said. 'Take a look at this.'

Trevor and Mike closed in as Kendra and Amir stepped back to give them room in the tight space.

'See here? It's faint, but there is a CCTV camera covering the rear exits, shops and flats alike, three of them. Additionally, I spotted at least one more here,' he said, tapping the monitor in one corner. 'The takeaway has built an extension of sorts in the yard, probably to store their foodstuff. If you look at the corner here, you can see another camera, which pretty much covers the whole yard. Amir is going to have problems getting in and doing his thing.'

The yard was tight and could fit two or three vehicles at

most. At this time there was only one, a dark saloon of indeterminate make. The space for vehicles was an L-shape, due to the takeaway's extension in one corner that ran the length of the yard and the width of the shop. In the opposite corner was another square, shed-like wooden structure, twice as wide as the takeaway's but half as long, allowing room for a vehicle to come into what was a paved courtyard suitable for two; three, if you were to block the entrance. There was also a tree and a large bush against the wall between the two structures. Amir took it all in and nodded, happy with what he'd seen.

'Don't worry about me,' he said confidently, 'now that I've seen the layout of the yard, I don't need to go in it via the access road. I'll go around it and climb. The cameras won't pick me up.'

'You can do that?' Mike asked, never having seen Amir's parkour skills.

'If only you knew what this guy can do, you'd wanna pay me a transfer fee so you can add him to your crew,' Trevor laughed, 'and it would be a world-record fee, I assure you.'

'Ah, that's good of you to say, Trev,' Amir said, offering Kendra's dad a fist to touch. Trevor ignored it.

'Don't get ahead of yourself, young man. You have a job to do, remember?'

'Received and misunderstood, sir, yes sir,' Amir replied enthusiastically, in his usual exaggerated manner. He gave a mock salute and left the camper van, carrying the kit that would make the team's job easier.

'You may as well bring Mabel back,' Kendra told Andy. 'Now that we've seen the cameras, best leave Amir to it.'

'Mabel?' Mike said.

'Don't ask,' Trevor replied, shaking his head.

As it was late, there were few on the streets. The hair salon and grocery shop were closed, and the fried chicken takeaway had one solitary customer at the counter waiting for his late evening meal. Amir approached the neighbouring construction site where an office block was being renovated. There was extensive scaffolding in place as well as skips and building materials that gave him plenty of cover.

He gave a casual look over his shoulder to see if anyone was watching him before smartly jumping up and grabbing a scaffolding pole. It took just a few seconds for the skilled parkourist to shimmy up to the first level, where wooden planks had been laid. The scaffolding was sheathed in a mesh screen which acted as a wind breaker as well as preventing debris from falling onto passers-by. After another quick look, Amir continued along the boards towards the back of the building, which overlooked the yard he was aiming for.

'So far, so good,' he whispered. He could see the faint red lights on each of the CCTV cameras, which helped him to pinpoint them in the dark. Working his way to the end, he determined where he wanted to land and quickly leapt from the scaffolding down onto the narrow brick wall surrounding the yard. He held his arms out for balance, before crouching and then dropping down silently into the yard, using the large bush for cover. Taking a GPS tracker from his pocket, he lay flat on his stomach and worked his way slowly towards the parked car, a dark blue Lexus SUV, using it to shield him from the cameras, and wedged the tag between the silver trim and the bumper.

He squirmed back to the bush the same way he'd left it,

on his stomach, before taking stock and ensuring the coast was still clear. Next, he took a small, covert surveillance camera that the team had used so successfully in the past, and placed it between two branches of the tree, facing the back of the shops. He made sure it was secure by adding a globule of industrial, quick-drying glue.

The next step was for another camera, which meant being exposed for longer than he was comfortable with, by crawling quickly towards the extension and then part-way along the top of the extension itself. When he got to where he was aiming for, he smiled and proceeded to place another small camera directly next to the one the bad guys had installed. Again, he made sure to secure it with the glue.

Before leaving, he glanced up at the flats above the shops and did a double take.

'Mo?' he whispered to himself, when he saw a partial silhouette of a man moving around in the top-floor flat. Amir took a chance and stood up to get a better view into the flat. He could see the silhouetted figure walking back and forth, as if on guard, and figured that his brother must be nearby.

Bastards! he thought, as he took in the surroundings, noting where the downpipes were, the width of the window ledges, what sort of windows they were, everything he needed to know before making his plans. He then ducked down and headed back towards the rear wall, before taking cover behind the tree once more.

Amir wasn't happy that the two cameras he'd placed covered only the yard and the doors. He could see only one option, and that was *up*. This wasn't the tallest tree he'd climbed, but it was tall enough that he could see the windows on the second floor more clearly. He retrieved another camera and placed it on a branch, butting it up against the trunk and securing it with more glue, making sure to position it for the best possible angle of view. Only when he was happy did he make his way back down.

As he retraced his steps to safety, Amir took one last look behind his shoulder.

'Stay strong, brother, we're coming for you,' he whispered.

Three minutes later he was back with Andy, Kendra, Trevor, and Mike in the back of Marge.

'Great job, Amir, all three cameras are working just fine,' Andy said, giving him a thumbs-up.

'Good, now can we go and get my brother?'

'*Standby, standby,*' the commando said into his radio as the entry team readied themselves.

'*Relay, standby, standby,*' the team leader repeated.

'*Go, go, go!*' came the command.

Two colleagues in black night gear, including balaclavas and tactical helmets, approached the front door and smashed into it with the purpose-built battering ram. Their first blow was aimed in the vicinity of the door lock and handle, which would usually splinter with one or two blows. Failing that, they would attack the hinges. The door never stood a chance and gave way with the first massive blow. The two men moved swiftly out of the way to allow three other colleagues to enter the flat at speed, surprise being the aim.

'Armed police, armed police, put your hands up, now!' screamed the first commando as they came across the two men in the living room, watching an episode of Columbo.

The two men obliged, shocked at the sudden, violent intrusion, and never even considered that the commandos weren't police at all and that they wouldn't be taken to the local police station they were so familiar with.

They were both manhandled into a standing position and swiftly searched by their captors. The team leader approached the elder of the two, his hands now zip-tied behind his back.

'I'm only going to ask you once. Where are the guns?'

'I... I don't know what you're talking about,' the older man said, glaring at the masked man.

The team leader took a stun gun out of its pouch on his belt and pressed it against the man's neck, instantly shocking him. He collapsed to the ground, coughing and spluttering in shock.

'The next one will be twice as long, and so on. Where are the guns?' the team leader asked calmly, the stun gun now back at the prisoner's neck and waiting for the next shock. The man knew not to argue any further.

'We... we just have t-two,' he said, indicating to the kitchen with his head, knowing full well he was not going to win this one. 'I... in the cupboard under the sink. The... the others are at a lock-up.'

The team leader gestured towards the kitchen for one of his men to check. The man returned seconds later with the holdall, nodding. They had found the guns.

'What else is here?' asked the team leader, again placing the stun gun against the man's neck.

'Noth... nothing, I sw-swear!' the man said.

The team leader went to the front door, where one man was standing guard, just inside and out of view from anybody walking past.

'Do a rough search of the flat, turn it upside down if you have to. Do it quick. I'll stand guard,' he said, and they swapped places. He took out a phone and called the First Sea Lord. 'Both men in custody, sir, and two rifles secure.'

'Well done, Sergeant. Take them to the secure area and prepare them for questioning,' the admiral replied.

AT THE PARKWOOD Industrial Estate in Maidstone, another armed unit was gaining entry into storage unit 150 on the first floor. The rifles were quickly found, secured, and removed to a waiting van before being taken back to the base. The team leader at this location called the First Sea Lord to provide an update on their progress.

'Sir, the rifles have been recovered and all traces have been removed from the unit,' the captain said.

'Thank you, Captain. How many rifles did you secure?'

'We counted eighty, sir.'

'Shit!'

'THAT'S NOT GOOD,' Trevor said. 'So we have, what, fifteen missing?'

'That's correct. It might not sound like many, but fifteen of those rifles can do an awful lot of damage, Trevor,' said Sir Robert. 'We need to find them, and fast.'

'Have you picked up the armourer yet?' Trevor asked. 'Maybe he can tell you where they are.'

'The team are on their way to pick him up now, they wanted to wait until the early hours to avoid detection,' the admiral said. 'I hope you're right and that he can tell us.'

'Let me know when you hear back, sir; we have a man to rescue here so I need to go and make that happen.'

'Be careful, Trevor, remember how much damage they can do,' Sir Robert said.

'That sounded slightly ominous, fifteen missing rifles?' Kendra said, 'do they think the gangs have stashed them here?'

'No idea, love; there's only one way to find out, and that's to go in tonight. We need to rescue poor Mo before it's too late and find out if they have any of the rifles here.' Trevor's expression was grim as he considered the potential consequences of rushing in.

'May I interject?' Andy said, his hand up in the air as if asking a question in class.

'Sure, what is it?' Kendra replied.

'Well, you know that email I sent from Land Registry, the one with the virus embedded?'

'What about it?' asked Trevor.

'One of those wonderful gangster people just opened it.' Andy smirked.

'What are we looking at? It looks like gibberish to me,' Kendra said.

'That *gibberish*, as you call it, is the program making progress in the computers in those very buildings we are watching,' he said smugly.

'So, you have access to them?' asked Trevor.

'Once the program has run its course, yes. I can then take over their CCTV system, block any phone numbers that are registered to them here, and do some major damage to their bank accounts. Should take an hour or so and I'll be able to start, but it may be a problem if someone is monitoring the computers as they can power them down and stop me from doing what I need to do. You'll have to coincide your efforts to rescue Mo and use it as a distraction for me to do my thing.'

'So, we have to wait an hour?' Amir asked. 'They could be beating the hell out of him as we speak, we need to go now!'

'Amir, maybe it's time to put your skills to use and go solo until we're ready,' Trevor said. 'Can you gain entry into that room where you think he might be?'

'I know I can, but there's bound to be someone there with him. I saw someone pacing, remember?'

'The light has gone out in that room, maybe they've gone to bed or something,' Andy said.

'I'll go and take a look,' Amir said. 'If it's clear and I can see Mo, I'll gain entry and keep him safe until the cavalry arrives.'

'Sounds like a plan, just be careful. Take some kit with you for Mo, you may need it,' Trevor added.

'ARE you sure this is going to work, Amir?'

'I wouldn't be doing it if I didn't think it would work, Kendra, would I? And I'm willing to take chances if it means getting my brother out of there safely.'

'But you'll be on your own,' she added, 'nobody can help you for about an hour. I just want to be sure you've thought this through.'

'Look, you and the team need to get into the building and take it over, we've agreed on that much, right? When you go in, what do you think is going to happen? It'll be all hands to the pump, those bastards will all make their way to head you off. They won't leave anyone to check on a prisoner, more likely tie him to a bed or something, so it'll be easy. Honestly, don't worry, just do your thing and leave Mo to me.'

'Okay, but you make sure to keep in touch at all times, okay?'

'I will, Kendra, I promise. Now, go and join the rest of them and let me get into position. I'll see you soon,' he said, giving a mock salute before disappearing out of sight.

14

RESCUE

Ex-armourer Reg Malone was fast asleep in his luxury static caravan in East Malling and did not see the soft glow of the plasma torch that cut through his lock like a knife through butter. Neither did he see the four dark-clothed men that entered, one of whom covered Reg's mouth with a mask while the other two held him down. Instinctively, Reg inhaled and took a dose of anaesthetic, which rendered him unconscious in a matter of seconds.

Two of the men carried him to the van that had arrived as they'd made their entry, and he was quickly bundled into the back. While he was being sedated and then carried out, the two other men were searching through the accommodation for any firearms that may have been stashed there, with no luck. The entry, sedation, search of the caravan and the removal of Reg Malone took less than three minutes. There weren't many of Reg's caravan park neighbours around at this time of the year, so nobody saw or heard a thing as he was whisked away to a secure location for what was likely to be a harsh interrogation.

The team leader for this operation called the admiral to update him.

'Any trace of rifles?' the admiral asked.

'No, sir, nothing here,' the sergeant replied.

'Shit.'

AMIR RETRACED his steps and climbed the scaffolding as he had done earlier. The takeaway was also closed now, so there was nobody around to witness the athletic twin make the jump across to the wall again. He moved swiftly across the extension and reached the rear wall by the down pipe that he intended to climb. He was relieved to see that it was an old metal one, meaning it would take his weight better than the newer, lighter plastic ones. He grabbed hold and started to climb, aiming for the second-storey window at the end of the building, now in darkness.

Hold on, brother, he thought, as he came level with the window. There was a gap of almost six feet, so Amir climbed slightly higher to allow for his jump to be of a slightly downward trajectory, giving him a better chance of hitting his mark. He took a deep breath and leapt.

Amir sighed with relief as he grabbed the sill and held on, spreading his weight on the brickwork below. He pulled himself up slowly, levering himself onto the sill and resting on his knees as he held his breath, listening for any hazards. He could hear nothing, so he turned his attention to the window. He smiled when he saw that it hadn't been locked, very common for a window two storeys and thirty-odd feet up. It was a sash window, almost a hundred years old, so it would likely make a noise when he tried to open it. He took out his penknife and stuck it into the wood in the middle of the bottom frame. With some force, he made sure the knife was well embedded and secure before he slowly began to lift it, taking the window with it.

As he opened the window slowly, a quiet scraping noise could be heard, and Amir prayed that there was nobody hostile in the room. Suddenly, the window was opened fully, and Amir was grabbed and hauled inside. Strangely, he landed on a mattress that lay on the floor underneath the window and there was very little noise from his landing. A hand covered his mouth, holding him down.

'What kept you, brother?'

'Mo? You didn't just do that, did you?' Amir whispered angrily as his eyes acclimatised to the moonlit room. He sat up and grabbed his brother tight.

Mo could only return the hug with one arm, as the other was handcuffed to the radiator below the window.

'I knew you'd come,' he said, beaming. 'I heard you climbing the pipe and thought I'd surprise you. Those bastards are in a room at the other end, there's a bathroom next door and then a kitchen, so nobody will have heard a thing. In fact, if you listen, you can hear them talking, they're watching some Asian films and acting out the martial arts, I think.'

'How many are there?'

'Five of them brought me here, and there were three already here. There's another two bedrooms, one being used as an office, and the lounge at the end. So, eight altogether, and they have guns.'

'Sweet, just give me a second.' Amir took out his phone.

'Hi, Kendra. I'm in and with Mo, he's fine but handcuffed to a radiator. There are eight hostiles here, armed, so be aware when you enter. The flat has three bedrooms, one used as an office, one at the end where Mo is being held, a lounge where most of them are at the moment, and a kitchen. I'm gonna try and get these cuffs off my brother and will hold the hostiles off if they come checking, don't worry.'

He rang off, before reaching into a pocket and removing two plastic wedges.

'These should hold them off until it's too late for them to do any more harm,' he said, placing them underneath the door, one at each end. 'Now, let me look at those cuffs.'

Mo had been secured using police-style handcuffs, so Amir was confident he could remove them. He took out a small pouch, removing an L-shaped tool that he then inserted into the keyhole of the cuffs.

'You still carry that around with you, eh?' Mo grinned.

'It helps to be prepared, brother,' Amir said, listening for the tell-tale click as he slowly twisted the implement. He smiled when he heard the distinctive noise and the cuffs came open, freeing his brother.

'Good job, Amir, thank you,' Mo said, rubbing his wrist. 'Now, are we supposed to wait for the team?'

'We could always go back the way I came.'

'I may not be as skilled at parkour as you, but I can climb down a bloody pipe,' Mo said, looking out of the window. 'Although that is a fair way.'

'Just do what I do, you'll be fine.' Amir stepped out onto the sill, holding onto the window frame for support. He leapt effortlessly, dropping towards the down pipe, grabbing on with both hands and placing his legs either side. Looking up at his brother, he shimmied back down to the roof of the extension.

'He makes it look so damned easy, the show-off,' Mo muttered as he assumed the position on the sill. 'Here goes nothing.'

He leapt for the pipe, grabbing hold with one hand and slamming into the wall, which was somewhat painful, before quickly grabbing with both and hanging ungainly before shimmying down.

'Stop laughing,' he said as he joined Amir on the extension. Amir was trying hard not to laugh.

'I wish I'd recorded that,' he said, as they started to make their way back towards the rear of the property.

Amir retraced his steps, and they climbed down into the side access road, confident that nobody would spot them at this time of night. Amir led his brother away from his former prison and to safety, making a call to Kendra when they were clear.

'Mo is safe, we'll be with you shortly.'

'Great stuff, Amir. See you soon, we're getting ready to go in.'

'Good, 'coz I don't want to miss that,' he replied.

KENDRA GAVE Mo a big hug when he entered the camper van, quickly followed with much of the same from Trevor and Andy.

'I must admit, we were a little worried,' Kendra said. 'It's so good to have you back in one piece. Are you hurt?'

'Just a few bruises. They were waiting on the big boss to

turn up and torture me, or something, so it was good timing getting me out.' Mo squeezed his brother's arm.

'So, there's only eight of them in the flat?' asked Trevor.

'I'm pretty sure of that,' said Mo. 'The stairs from the yard lead to the left side of the building and come out near the lounge, so they had to bring me past each of the rooms before they locked me in the end bedroom. The one next to the lounge looks to be set up as an office, with a couple of computers and filing cabinets, and I saw two Asian men working there. The five guys that brought me here were three east Africans and two Bengalis. A couple of them kept arguing so I'm guessing they're from two separate gangs and that's all that's left of them.'

'That's some great intel, Mo, great work. That suggests this is just one place they work from and I'm guessing the main players from the Vietnamese gang are currently elsewhere.'

'So, do we wait? Or go in as planned?' Andy asked. 'It's just that my program is done so I can go in and start causing them some damage.'

'Are you sure about this, Dad? If they've got the rifles, I don't think we should risk it.'

'I don't know how else we can do this, love. We need the distraction so Andy can get into their systems without being noticed.' Trevor shrugged.

'You need a distraction? I think I can do something about that,' said Amir. 'It means going back, but I'm pretty sure they have no idea yet that Mo has escaped.'

'What are you thinking, brother? I'm not a fan of the idea of you going back,' Mo said.

'Don't worry, I'll be in and out in a couple of minutes and

they won't have a clue what's happening. I just need some lighter fuel and a newspaper and I'm good to go.'

'Okay, Amir, make sure to stay on the phone as you're doing your thing, we need to time this perfectly,' Kendra said, when Amir had called from the room from which he had helped his brother escape.

'No problem, Kendra. I can still hear them pretending to be Bruce Lee, so tell Andy to get ready, as I'm about to start some chaos.'

He took the rolled-up newspaper from his inside jacket pocket and lay it flat on the floor. He then soaked the first half of the paper with the lighter fuel, and left a thin trail to the rear half, before slowly pushing it underneath the door. The two wedges were still in place so if anyone happened upon his antics, he'd likely have time to make his escape before they gained entry. When he was happy with the positioning, he lit the fuel trail and watched as the fire followed the fuel and to the half that was soaked. Having done it many times, Amir knew that the flames would burn the outer side of the door quickly, melting the paint and creating a thick, pungent smoke that would soon catch the attention of the gang. He didn't have to wait long.

'Fire! The bastard has started a fire!' Imran Aziz shouted to the others when he went to check on the smell.

'What? How did he do that? He's handcuffed to the bloody radiator!' said Raheem Abdi.

The three Vietnamese men came out to join them from the next room and started shouting in their mother tongue.

'Get water from kitchen and put it out!' one man shouted.

Amir had heard the commotion and spoke into the phone.

'Did you get that, Kendra? Time to make myself scarce, tell Andy to hurt them badly,' he said, making his way back to the window and making a hasty exit.

'Loud and clear, Amir. Now get the hell out of there,' she said. The phone was silent; Amir had already left the building.

'Already on it, K,' Andy said, having overheard the conversation. 'I only need thirty seconds or so to upload the program I need, so as long as they're not looking at the screen, they won't have a clue.' His fingers flew across the keyboard.

'Great. They're in for a shock when they get through that door,' she said.

'As long as Amir is safely away, then we've succeeded in one part, but we still need to take these bastards out at some point,' Trevor reminded them.

'I suggest we start planning for all eventualities,' said Andy, 'because it won't take long before they find out what I've done. You won't believe how much money these animals have stashed away.'

15

VIRUS

Amir entered the rear of the camper van to an unusual sight: Trevor, Kendra, and Mike all staring at Andy, open-mouthed.

'How much, did you say?' Trevor asked.

'Eighteen million pounds and some change, spread over four bank accounts. That's what they have now, but I can tell you they've had a lot more, which they send regularly to accounts overseas that I won't be able to access.'

'Can you grab these funds?' Kendra asked.

'Not at the moment, we need to have access to the main man's phone, because any transfers will require two-factor authentication, which will go through his phone. I can see there is only one number that controls that, and it's likely to be Kam's.'

'Shit, how can we get access to his phone if he's not even here?' asked Trevor.

'I think I know a way. I can see all the files on their property portfolio, which is extensive. They already have five hotels all over the country and about a dozen bed-and-break-fast properties, along with sixteen houses and a dozen cash-only businesses like nail salons, takeaways, brothels, and car-cleaning firms. I know what they're doing now, it's plain to see with the documents I've downloaded.'

'What is it?' Trevor asked.

'They're loan sharks who are doing everything they can to make people default so they can take over business and property. They then use the properties to house illegal immigrants, many of whom come over from Vietnam, to work for next to nothing. Basically, they're using forced labour and making a fortune; it's a nasty but efficient way of making a profit in all their own businesses as well as charging rent for the privilege of housing their own workers. And, of course, they don't pay tax, or much of anything else.'

'How the hell do they get away with something like that?' Mike Romain asked.

'There's so many people coming over nowadays that the authorities just can't keep up. I think there's something like three thousand people a month coming over by boat from France alone, let alone into airports and seaports. Most of the efforts are spent on trying to stop them coming in; they don't tend to do much once they're here, so bastards like Kam can exploit them without fear of capture,' Kendra said, knowing full well the extent of the problem.

'How do we get this guy, Kam, Andy? What do you need to get access to his phone?' Trevor asked.

'Well, now that I have the number, I need to figure out how to contact him without him becoming suspicious. I'll trawl through the bank statements and see if there are any transactions that would seem suspicious enough for a bank to call and confirm. Once I get him on the phone, I can upload the program that will give me access to it.'

'Do what you can, mate, we need to sort this lot out. They're making a bloody fortune off the back of slavery, is what they're doing,' Trevor said angrily.

It was broad-shouldered Raheem who finally smashed his way into the room, splintering the wooden door frame.

'Where the hell is he?' Imran asked.

'He's escaped, you fool!' Raheem gestured to the open window. He went over to take a look; on the off chance they might be able to see anything. The empty cuff was still attached to the radiator. Their prisoner was long gone.

'He must have had something on him to free himself with,' Raheem said. 'It doesn't matter now; he's gone, so we need to go look for him before the boss finds out. Having the prisoner was going to save us, remember? Now, we have nothing, he's going to be pissed... really pissed.'

'Before we do this, there's something else you should know,' Andy said.

'What's that?' Trevor asked.

'The guys that work out of this flat are Kam's lawyer and accountants, whose jobs are to maintain the records, transfer monies, and make sure everything is legal on paper. I saw one document that mentions the deeds to all the properties, and they are all stored in the safe, which I can only assume is in that office.'

'If we can get those deeds as well as the money, we can

destroy them financially,' Kendra said, 'but how do we do that when they're armed to the teeth?'

'We can't think about that now, let's focus on Kam and the bank accounts. Once we have that sorted out, then we can worry about everything else. Remember, we still have prisoners and probably this lot to deal with,' Trevor said, referring to the eight gang members languishing in the secure rooms back at the factory.

'I'd forgotten about them,' Kendra said.

'They're in good hands; Greg and Danny are looking after them. They're lacing the food and drinks with sleeping pills, so they're nicely sedated,' Trevor said.

'We need to renegotiate our fee, Trevor,' Mike joked, 'especially if you get your hands on that money!'

'Before you ask, whatever money we take from criminals pays for everything and also goes back to the victims or the community,' Trevor said, 'but I'm sure we can renegotiate. For example, how about the purchase of your company?'

Mike was stunned. 'Are you serious? You'd buy my company?'

'Why not? It's a no-brainer, isn't it? Your surveillance skills are excellent, and they will enhance the legitimate part of our operation significantly. Sherwood Solutions is growing, Mike, and you'd be a great asset to us. Think about it.'

'Guys, sorry to interrupt, but we should think about moving away until we can go to the next phase,' Kendra reminded them. 'Andy can't make the call to Kam at this time of the night, and there's nothing to be done here that the cameras and GPS tag can't tell us. I suggest we get some rest until the morning.'

'I'll stand the team down for now,' Mike said. 'What time will you be making the call?'

'It can only be during opening hours,' said Andy, 'so I suggest calling just after nine tomorrow morning.'

'Okay, thanks. I'll have my team on the plot by then in case there's any movement. We'll cover it loosely until we get a firm contact with the main target,' Mike added.

'Okay, mate, see you in the morning,' said Trevor. 'Let's get out of here, team. Kendra, call the others and tell them to get back to the factory. Someone can relieve Danny and Greg and then we'll make our way back here in the morning before you make that call.'

'Mo, are you okay to drive? I want to see what else Andy has downloaded, it may help us sort this lot out quicker,' Kendra said.

'Sure, no problem.'

'Should we get Rick involved in this?' Andy asked.

'Maybe later; he's got his hands full with the arrests at the hotel. I'll update him about our progress in the morning,' Kendra said, turning to her father, who was looking at his phone and shaking his head. 'What's wrong, Dad?'

'Shit. I just got a message from the admiral. They've recovered the rifles from the storage unit and from those two yobs, but there's still fifteen missing. We must assume that this lot have them, or Kam has. Either way, things are likely to get very tense until we can recover the missing weapons.'

'Let's revisit this tomorrow, there's nothing we can do tonight,' Kendra said.

They left the area and headed for the factory, knowing that their job was hanging in the balance. Even if they succeeded in grabbing the funds from the criminals, if the rifles were still out there, it would not give them much comfort.

'I've seen what those rifles are capable of. There's a reason why the marines picked them, so I can't imagine the harm they will do in the wrong hands,' Trevor said.

Kendra placed a hand on his arm, but had no words, knowing that his fear was very real.

THE TEAM REASSEMBLED in the morning, rested and ready to be briefed about the impending danger posed by the missing rifles being in the hands of some very dangerous people.

'Every one of you must wear your tactical vests and take additional gear with you in the event we need to make an entry into that or another building, so make sure to check each other, okay?' Kendra told them.

'We'll keep you updated as and when we locate the rest of them, so in the meantime, be sure to park far enough away until we call you in,' Trevor added.

'We'll also have a surveillance team to help with any follows, in case you see anyone plotted up around the vicinity. If you do, then it means you're too close, so move farther away,' Kendra said. 'Stay safe, everyone.'

The team dispersed, all heading off back to the previous night's location. It was clear there were some nerves, but there was also a determination that Kendra saw in the team, giving her confidence.

'Call Rick and give him the heads-up, love,' Trevor said. 'I'll wait for you in the van with Andy.'

'Will do. I shan't be long,' she replied, calling Rick.

'How's it going, K? Will we see you today, or are you still off?' Rick said, referring sarcastically to the schedule that Kendra was keeping as a part-time operative on his team. In other words, she came in whichever days suited her, and as long as she made up the minimum number of days required, nobody questioned it.

'It's all good, Rick. Just wanted to let you know that Mo is safe, and that there are fifteen rifles still unaccounted for after last night's raids. We're hoping to locate them today, all being well. How's it going on your end?'

'It's been a long couple of days, as you can imagine. The arseholes have all been interviewed and we'll be charging them today with a variety of charges, ranging from firearms offences to attempted murder. The exciting part is done, it's the boring shit now, so you're lucky to be away.'

'Understood. That lot are the lucky ones, they'll get a chance to sample His Majesty's prison food and have a nice comfy bed every night. The lot that we're after won't be so lucky,' she said, 'and hopefully a lot poorer. I'll call later to update you when we know what's happening.'

'Understood. If I can get away, I'll try and come to help, but if not, you know why. The paperwork we still have to do is a friggin' nightmare.'

'I'd normally feel guilty, but in this case, I think I'll just say farewell and good luck!'

After hanging up the phone, she went to join Andy and Trevor, who both waited in the rear of Marge, their trusted mobile operations van.

'Looks like you're driving, love, and let's get a move on. Andy here has an important call to make.'

'OKAY, everyone is in position, it's time to make the call,' Kendra said, handing Andy the burner phone he had prepared the previous night to register as a bank number.

'Just a word of warning, I'm going to talk in my posh voice, so don't laugh!'

Dialling Kam's number, he looked up at his monitor to make sure everything was in order for him to work from.

'Yes?'

'Good morning, sir. This is Barclays Bank calling, Muswell Hill branch, and my name is Edwin Harlan, from the premier business account department, one of the managers on your account. Am I speaking with Mr Raymond Kam of Legacy Solutions?'

'You are. What is the purpose of this call?'

'I'm sorry to bother you, Mr Kam. I'm calling to ask about an irregular transaction from your premier account that we need to confirm before it is authorised. Before I discuss further, may I ask you some security questions, sir?'

Kam paused before answering.

'Why do you need to ask me security questions? You have called me, so tell me what the transaction is, and I will confirm whether it is genuine or not.'

'I'm afraid I can't do that, sir, the bank policy is to confirm your identity before I can disclose any information. Do you have the bank app downloaded to your phone? If so, then another way to verify your identity is to click on a message that I can send to your phone now, as you are registered in the system and your identity can be verified,' Andy said.

'One minute,' Kam said, swearing in his native tongue before continuing, 'go ahead and send it.'

'Sending now, sir. Just click on the link in the message and I will receive confirmation,' Andy said.

'There, I have clicked it,' Kam grumbled.

'Thank you, Mr Kam, your check is verified. I am calling about a transaction made yesterday for the amount of seventeen thousand pounds to Magellan Autos Limited. Did you make that transaction, sir?' Andy asked.

'Yes, I did. That is the deposit on a new Mercedes, it is legitimate,' Kam replied.

'Thank you, Mr Kam, that is good to hear. The payment made will not be investigated further. Is there anything else I can do for you today?'

'No,' Kam replied, and ended the call abruptly.

'That was a tad rude, wasn't it?' Andy said, turning to Trevor and Kendra with a wicked, knowing grin.

'Did it work?' Kendra asked.

'Oh, yes. The worm is now feasting on his phone's innards, and he won't have a clue.' Andy leaned back smugly, hands behind his head.

'How long will it take before you can clone his phone?' asked Trevor.

'It usually takes a few hours, but we have to be careful and know when to make a move. Ideally it should be left overnight, but if we keep track of where he is, we may get an indication of whether we have time. I need about fifteen minutes to clear everything out of the bank accounts.'

'How will we get an indication?' Kendra asked.

'One of the things I added to the phone is a tracker, so we'll know exactly where he is, what calls he makes, what messages he sends or receives, the works. When I'm ready, I'll be able to block his phone, but use the clone to make the transactions, as the banks will send two-factor authentication codes to the phone, which I'll need to confirm the transfers.'

'Man, you make it sound so easy. Surely it isn't?' Trevor asked.

'No, not really. This extra layer of security has stopped a huge amount of fraud, but a handful of us are skilled enough to get around those measures and make it work. Obviously, it helps that I find ways to upload works and viruses; not many people can do that without detection. So, I figure why not, eh? It's one of my favourite ways of making the baddies pay for their crimes, literally!'

'I've said this before, and I'll say it again, I hope I never end up on your bad side,' Trevor said, patting Andy on the back. 'Just don't get too cocky, okay? Let's remember that there's some nasty weaponry out there that we need to find; hopefully his phone will help with that too.'

16

POTTERS BAR

'We've got some movement in the back yard,' Andy said. 'It looks like the five remaining gang members are having a chat of sorts. That big fella is getting very animated.'

They watched as the five men seemed to argue in the yard, before things calmed down and everyone stood still as the largest of the five made a phone call.

'Oh, stand by,' Andy said, spotting movement on another monitor, 'chummy in the yard is calling Kam, look.'

The screen that Andy had dedicated to monitoring Kam's phone was flashing to indicate an incoming call.

'Can we listen in?' Kendra asked.

'Not without risking discovery, no, it could cause problems if they're using an encrypted app, which may flag up two phones and set off all sorts of alarms for him. The system I have set up allows me to block his phone, so all calls and messages, and intercept them on the cloned phone. Also, I can track his location, so we'll know where he is at all times.'

'Shame, it would be good to know what they're talking about,' Trevor said.

'Also, remember, I can track the gang's phones, too, using a very different program. I can't intercept their calls or do anything other than see where they are, like a GPS tag,' Andy added.

'I'm not complaining, that is excellent intelligence by any standard; knowing where the targets are is always a good thing,' Kendra said. 'It will be interesting to see what those five do now that they've lost their prisoner.'

'Kam has answered; look, it's stopped flashing,' Andy said.

They turned to the other monitor and saw the larger of the men on the phone, gesturing animatedly.

'Oh, to be a fly on the wall,' Andy said.

'WHAT DO YOU MEAN, he's escaped?'

'He climbed out of the second-storey window, Mr Kam,' said Raheem, nervously. 'I don't know how he got free of the cuffs, but now he's gone. What do you want us to do?'

There was a pause as Kam considered his reply.

'I want you to stay and protect my men, in case the bastard comes back with more of his friends. We need to clear everything out of the flat and take everything to another location.'

'We can do that, sir. Where will we take everything? And can we have more of the rifles?'

'There are three rifles in the Lexus, take those and await my instructions,' Kam said. 'No more screw-ups, Raheem, do you hear me?'

'I hear you, sir. Your men will be safe, you have my word,' the Deptford Mafia leader replied.

'WHAT ARE THEY DOING?' Kendra asked as she saw the men go to the rear of the dark blue Lexus, on which Amir had placed the GPS tag.

'Is that what I think it is?' asked Trevor. 'Andy, can you zoom in?'

They had opened the rear hatch to the SUV and lifted the carpet, revealing a compartment beneath where the spare tyre should have been. The larger of the men had looked around to make sure he wasn't being watched before taking out a rifle from the compartment and passing it to one of the other men, who quickly hid it underneath his jacket. The man repeated this twice more before replacing the carpet and closing the rear hatch.

'I counted three, it looks like that's all there was in there,' Kendra said.

'Agreed. That leaves twelve more, which we can now assume are in Kam's control. I need to inform the admiral,' Trevor said, stepping back to message the First Sea Lord.

'They're all going back into the flat,' Andy said. 'I'm guessing they're reinforcing in case Mo comes back for a spot of revenge.'

'Are they Kam's men?' Kendra asked, as she saw two more men exit the flat and go to the SUV, carrying boxes that they placed in the rear. The men returned and made several more trips, loading up the Lexus.

'None of them look big enough for the rifles,' Trevor said,

'which means they're clearing out everything in case they do have a visit. Damn, this could be a stumbling block for us.'

'Not necessarily, Dad. Remember, we have a tracker on that car so we'll know exactly where it ends up, which could be where the rifles are being stored.'

'Maybe, but I really wanted those deeds and everything to do with the properties and businesses they've acquired. Who knows what they'll do with them now.'

'I don't think we'll have long to wait,' Andy said. 'It may be worth warning Mike and the team that there's likely to be some movement very soon.'

Two of the Deptford Mafia crew left the flat and walked towards the road, away from the building. Trevor took his phone out and made a call.

'Mike, we have two of the gang members out, on foot, away from the building towards Victoria Road and out of our vision. There's a good chance they're heading for the Travelodge nearby, which is where they've been staying. Let your team know to be aware.'

'Will do. I have one of our footies nearby, I'll have them do a walk-by,' Mike replied.

'Thanks, mate, speak soon.'

A few minutes later, Mike called back.

'The two men are into a blue Audi A4 index Tango-golf-six-two-kilo-kilo-Victor, and away from the car park. Do you want us to follow?'

'No, let them go, we can track one of their phones if we need to,' Trevor said. 'Oh, hang on, the Audi just turned up here. It looks like they're readying to move out with our Vietnamese friends.'

The car had reversed into the courtyard, blocking the entrance, ahead of the SUV that had been loaded. The remaining three gang members came out of the flat, looking around warily, their awkward gait suggesting they were carrying the rifles under their jackets. Three Vietnamese men followed them, carrying briefcases and rucksacks, which they loaded into the SUV.

All five gang members got into the Audi and drove off slowly, followed by the Lexus.

'Okay, that's all eight from the flat. I'll call Darren and the team, and you call Mike back, Dad,' Kendra said. 'Andy, stay on the monitors and I'll drive your beloved Marge.'

Calls were made to the team, with instructions to stay well out of the way. Kendra stayed behind the following vehicles, with Trevor giving occasional updates to Darren and Mike to ensure everyone was aware of where they were heading.

Initially, they headed east along the A406 North Circular Road before turning off and heading north along the A1. An hour later, they approached the junction of the A1 and the dreaded M25 motorway.

'Heads-up, Mike, we're approaching the nightmare motorway that is the M25, I suggest you move up a little,' Trevor said, as Kendra repeated the warning to Darren.

'That's strange, they've turned in towards the service station there,' Andy said, 'but they've not stopped for fuel. They're driving through it and joining St Alban's Road and now across the bridge over the A1. Okay, now they've turned towards Potters Bar.'

The surveillance team shifted their positions and closed in as their targets approached a built-up area.

'It's now a left at the roundabout from Cecil Road and into Cranbourne Road, which looks like it's towards another industrial estate and a dead end,' Andy warned.

'Kendra, tell the team to stay out of there, leave it to Mike's team,' Trevor said.

'Will do.'

'Mike, it's over to you, mate. They're heading towards the end of the road where the industrial estate is.'

'Thanks, Trevor; one of our team has the vehicles in sight and will deploy on foot when they stop.'

'Be careful, Mike, if those rifles are there and they spot you, there will be hell to pay,' Trevor said.

'Received and understood, old friend. Let's go and find out, eh?'

'*CONTACT, contact to three-five, it's a stop, stop, stop outside unit five-delta, which is behind a vehicle repairs garage by a small car park. The unit is on two levels, with a light on in the solitary upstairs window as you look from the front. I can see three other vehicles in the car park in front of the unit, stand by for index numbers,*' the surveillance foot officer said.

'*Good job, three-five. Are you comfortable from your position?*' Mike asked.

'*Yes, yes. I'm on foot and have good cover, I can stay here for some time. Standby, I have vision on all five occupants from the Audi and three from the Lexus all into the unit, taking boxes from the Lexus inside. I can confirm there is no way out of the estate other than a reciprocal route, over.*'

'*All received. Go ahead with the index numbers, one-zero over.*'

'*First vehicle is a black Mercedes, echo-Zulu-seven-zero-whisky-alpha-hotel. Second vehicle is a silver BMW, Romeo-Yankee-six-nine-papa-Lima-November. Third vehicle is a silver*

Porsche Cayenne, foxtrot-golf-seven-two-Mike-echo-echo. Three-five out.'

Mike called Trevor and passed on the index numbers.

'I'll call Rick and see if he can get some checks done, but bear with us as it may take a while,' Trevor told him.

'Not a problem, my team have it well covered here. I'll wait for your instructions.'

'Kendra, can you do the honours, love? I want to check in with the team, so if you can get those numbers to Rick and give him an update, I'll do the same with the admiral,' Trevor said.

'I think we should get Amir to do his thing and get a camera on that unit, what do you think?' Andy asked.

'I'll speak to him. He loves things like this,' Kendra said.

17

INFILTRATION

'Rick, are you in the office? We need some checks on cars if you're free to assist?' Kendra asked her boss.

'Sure, message them over and I'll get on that now. How's it all going out there?'

'Mo's escape has spooked them into moving out of the flat and we've followed them to another industrial estate in Potters Bar. We think the remaining rifles are stored there but we have no idea of how many people are in the unit, so we're setting up some cameras with Amir,' she replied.

'I suppose that's progress, hopefully they'll all be in this one place, which should make it easier for us to take them down.'

'If they do have all those weapons in there, I won't be sending any of the team in, that's for sure. We may have to get our mates from the military to assist, I'm sure they can handle it much better than us, and there won't be a record of it, either.'

'It sounds like it's all under control on your end. We're

making good progress, too; a couple of the London gang members have caved and are telling us all sorts of horror stories about what their leaders have been up to. We should get some good convictions out of it and many more clear ups than I ever thought,' Rick said.

'Nice. I don't envy the paperwork but knowing that a bunch of nasty individuals won't be doing any more harm for a few years makes it all worthwhile, eh?'

'It certainly does. I'll get those checks to you shortly, K, keep me informed,' Rick said.

'Will do, boss, chat later.'

Kendra turned to her father, who had just finished a call of his own.

'Rick should get those checks back to us soon,' she said, 'is the admiral aware? If the weapons are here, Dad, shouldn't we get him to come and get them? We aren't as well-trained or equipped as his lot, and after how they dealt with the Chinese gangs a while back, I think they're perfect for this.'

'I agree, and have already primed him, don't worry. If we can confirm that Kam and his entire entourage are here, then the admiral's ninjas will be doing some overtime, for sure.'

'I guess there's no pressure on Amir, then.' Kendra smiled.

'Bro, will you please calm down and let me get ready? You know I can do this, and that I am more than aware of the danger, but please don't stress me out anymore,' Amir pleaded.

'How am I stressing you out?' Mo asked, 'I'm just helping you check your kit, that's all.'

Although he was confident that he'd be rescued, being

someone's prisoner had rattled Mo and he wasn't happy that his little brother was putting himself at risk again.

'Just promise you'll be careful, okay? I saw what this lot are about, Amir, and I'm only alive because they were waiting on the boss to question me. They don't care about anything or anyone, and that makes them dangerous.'

'I have all the kit on, bro, plus, do you honestly think they can catch me? Anyway, all I'm doing is placing a few cameras, it's not like I'm going in to take them all on,' Amir joked.

'I know you better than you think, and that's exactly what you'll do if the opportunity comes up. Just place the cameras and come straight back, otherwise I'll make sure you never eat another kebab again.' Mo laughed.

'Don't joke about kebabs, bro, you know better than that,' Amir said, puffing his chest out and flexing his arms akin to the Incredible Hulk as he got out of the car.

'I'll see you soon,' Mo said, giving a thumbs-up as his brother disappeared around a corner, dressed in the team's all-black kit, a protective vest under his jacket. He called Trevor.

'Amir is on his way, hopefully just to place the cameras, but you know what he's like, so tell Mike's footie to be aware.'

'Thanks, Mo, I will.'

AMIR HAD CHECKED the layout of the estate online and had found that the unit was in the bottom left-hand corner of the dead end, relatively remote compared with most other units, with only one other unit nearby and nothing overlooking it. His plan was to approach from the rear first to see what surprises were in store, using the cover that the Potters Bar

Brook provided, the stream that bordered the southern part of the estate. Following it along the bank allowed him to approach the rear of the unit and another car park not visible from the front, which was filled with several parked lorries and half a dozen containers, presumably filled with goods that the organisation was storing there. Amir looked for cameras, which he spotted on one of the corners of the building, one that covered the rear and one that covered the side. The back of the unit had a shutter-type loading bay that was locked, and the side had a double door that appeared locked. Amir assumed there were more cameras covering the front and the other side.

He moved to the fence that went around the estate and looked through to see where a good position for would be for one of Andy's cameras.

'This is as good as any place,' he muttered to himself.

Recognising that the cameras weren't covering the bottom end of the car park, he quickly climbed the fence and hid behind one of the containers. The middle two containers were in line with the rear shutters, so he attached two cameras on each, towards the rear, to ensure that at least one of them had good coverage. He then went to the end container that was in line with the side of the building and repeated the process; the camera he placed there had a good view of the side door.

It was then that he saw an opportunity he couldn't resist. The way the two cameras were positioned, up high and on the corner of the building, meant there was a significant blind spot in their coverage. Looking around to make sure it was clear, he sprinted across the ten yards of tarmacked surface and stopped at the corner before grabbing hold of the downpipe and climbing. As it was second nature to him, and considerably easier than using some of his parkour skills, it didn't take long to reach the nearest window, less than four feet away. He was able to lean over and look in, to an unoccupied storeroom.

Amir took out his trusted metal ruler, which he used for interior locks such as this, and made the jump across to the window look effortless. Keeping to one side and ensuring that the room was empty, he slid the thin ruler between the frame and the window and pushed at the simple mechanism on the handle to force it open. There was little noise as he pulled the window open and within seconds he was inside, landing quietly onto the carpeted floor within.

The room had shelving on three sides and low-level cabinets back-to-back in the centre of the room. The cabinets had a number of boxes stacked up on top.

Let's have a little looksie, shall we? he thought.

'Uh-oh, he's doing it again,' Andy said as the cameras went online.

'Who is doing what again?' Kendra asked.

'Look!' he said, pointing to the monitor.

Kendra watched as Amir climbed and then gained entry to the building.

'Shit. Who's going to tell Mo?'

Amir listened for a few minutes to the sounds coming from within the building. He heard occasional voices in a language he didn't recognise but which he assumed was Vietnamese, coming from somewhere close by, certainly from the first floor. He also heard laughing and raised voices, this time in English and with a London accent, coming from downstairs. Confident that there was no imminent danger, he decided to investigate further.

He started checking the shelves, where he noticed a large quantity of cleaning products on one end, mainly for cleaning cars and carpets. The shelving on the opposite wall was stacked up with bottles of Isopropyl alcohol, acrylic, gels, cuticle oil, base and topcoats and all the necessary accoutrements that nail salons use. The shelving between the two contained large quantities of food packaging and equipment such as slicers, mixers, food processors, and utensils. Amir was aware of the businesses that Kam's organisation had taken over and nodded in appreciation when he realised that they were also acting as a distribution hub for their own businesses, keeping everything in-house, away from prying eyes.

He looked back at the shelving with the nail salon products and a plan started to form in his head.

I'd better ask before I do anything, he thought, grinning in anticipation.

The low-level cabinets in the middle contained office supplies, mainly printer paper, inks, some spare computer monitors.

They're efficient, I'll give them that.

He then opened one of the boxes stacked on top and smiled as he realised that he'd found the boxes that had been evacuated from the flat he'd sprung Mo from.

'Jackpot!'

'He's where?' Mo asked, incredulous. Kendra had called to let him know of his brother's whereabouts.

'He climbed up and went in through a window,' she explained, disappointed that she'd lost the rock, paper, scissors match with Andy and Trevor to determine would tell him.

'That stupid git, honestly I don't know why I bother sometimes,' Mo said furiously, his raised voice a rare thing to hear. 'How the hell are we related? Why doesn't he ever, ever listen to me?'

'Sorry, Mo, I don't know what else to tell you. It's entirely up to your brother what happens next, we have no idea,' Kendra said.

'I'm gonna kill him, properly kill him this time, just wait and see,' he shouted.

'I'll let you know when we hear anything, Mo. I'll leave you to it,' she said, quietly hanging up.

'How long has he been in there now?' Trevor asked.

'Coming up to twenty minutes. I haven't seen any unusual activity, and the phones seem normal, not erratic, so I can only assume he's still okay,' Andy said, more in hope than anything else.

'Damn, that boy,' Trevor murmured.

'Oh, standby, standby, there he is,' Andy said, watching as Amir climbed out of the window, closing it behind him and then shimmying down the drainpipe.

'What's that on his back?' Kendra asked.

'It looks like something wrapped in a sheet.' Andy squinted as he tried to zoom in. Before he could do so, Amir had reached the bottom, taken a quick look around, and had then run towards the fence and out of sight.

'Thank God for that.' Trevor sighed in relief.

'I'll let Mo know,' Kendra said. She dialled the elder twin again, and quickly said, 'He's out safely and on the way back, thought you should know.'

'Thanks, Kendra, and sorry for shouting earlier, but just so you know, I will beat the crap out of him when this operation is over!'

18

JACKPOT!

Amir made his way safely to the team. He had taken a huge risk, but it had paid off. Despite the success he had just had, he was thinking ahead to the potential damage the team could inflict on Kam's organisation. He was still tweaking his plan when he opened the door to Marge and the serious faces within.

'Blimey, has someone died?' he asked as he saw the look on Kendra, Trevor and Andy's faces.

'No, but there's a solid chance that your life may be over soon when your brother gets hold of you,' Kendra said, arching her eyebrows.

'Please don't give me that look of disappointment, Kendra, you know what I'm like. I don't do it just for the fun of it. I always have a plan in mind, and this one is a bloody good one,' he said, dropping the bundle to the floor.

'What's that?' Trevor asked.

'That, my friend, is what you've been after all this time. It's the deeds to more than two dozen properties and businesses, legal documents, statements, everything you need to make some changes.' Amir grinned.

'What?' Kendra exclaimed, opening the sheet to reveal the bundle of documents. 'How the hell did you get hold of these?'

'The room I went into was where they stored the boxes from the flat, so I thought, when in Rome...'

'That's bloody good work, Amir; this should make things interesting. Andy, can you use these to transfer ownership? Like you did with the Eastwood flats in Hackney?' he asked, referring to the Russian oligarch's son who had planned to become prime minister after starting a race war a couple of years earlier.

'Yes, I most certainly can. I just need you to let me know who to transfer them to and I'll start the process.'

'You said you had a plan, Amir, is that what you meant?' Kendra asked.

'Part of it, yes. I also have another part that I think will help give Andy enough time to grab everything else, but if Mo is pissed at me now, he's gonna be a nightmare when I tell you what I need to do next.'

RAYMOND KAM WAS FURIOUS, pacing up and down the first-floor office, his lieutenants watching nervously as he thought of a way to salvage the situation.

'Nothing has gone to plan with this operation, has it? First, we lose most of the men we need for the London area, and as a result we're unlikely to gain ownership of the hotel, and now we've lost the west London office. The one thing I've tried to do is keep the police away from our operations, but now they are swarming around the men we've lost, the hotel, and probably the flat, now that you've let a prisoner escape. Someone will pay a heavy price for this!'

He slammed his fist down on the table.

'Sir, if I may make an observation,' one of the men said.

'Speak!'

'We were doing very well until the two gangs got overconfident, sir. Most of the blame must be placed on them, they have failed us badly.'

'I am not happy with them, that is certain, but until things calm down, even the few we have left will be of assistance. It would be prudent to have them close by so that we can feed them to the wolves, if it means giving us time to disappear.' Kam nodded as a plan came to him.

'Sir?'

'We keep them here, we make them feel important, and then when the time comes, which I am sure it will... we sacrifice them to the police so they can take the blame. Where are the rest of the weapons?'

'In the small storage room, sir, hidden under the foodstuffs. Only we know where they are hidden,' the man replied.

'Okay, good. They have three of them already, I want you to give them another two so they each have one. Do that now and ask their leaders to come and speak with me,' Kam ordered.

'Yes, sir,' the man replied, leaving the room.

'In the meantime, nothing changes, except that we continue to look for hotels in the London area. This is where we need to expand more quickly,' he told the other men in the room. 'I want nothing to stop our expansion, do you hear? Nothing!'

RAHEEM AND IMRAN were escorted to a meeting room, with a large round table with eight chairs. Four seats were occupied by Kam and his men, and it was he who indicated for them to sit at the table.

'Things have not gone well, gentlemen,' Kam told his guests.

'Tell us what you need us to do to put things right, sir,' Imran said quickly, wanting to show that he was willing to do anything to regain Kam's favour. He was fed up and disillusioned after the way Raheem had dealt with things.

Kam nodded appreciatively; his face was stern, and his hands clasped together.

'What I want you to do is to go back to the hotel that should have been in my possession by now, and leave a message that nobody will ever ignore,' Kam demanded.

'What message, sir?' Raheem asked, concerned they'd be going back to the scene where dozens of police had recently been.

'I want you all to go back and use the weapons I have given you to destroy the place. If I can't have it, then neither shall anybody else.'

'YOU WANT TO DO WHAT?' Mo asked, barely able to believe what he was hearing from his brother. He had spent several minutes shouting abuse and pushing Amir to get his message of anger and frustration out, just as Amir had expected.

'I want to go back into the unit and set a fire that will create a distraction for Andy to do his magic,' Amir said.

Mo shook his head in disbelief and paced back and forth along the pavement where he had parked the car. Amir had known his location and walked to find him, thankful there were no witnesses to his brother's outburst.

'Every time... you do this every time. Mum must have dropped you on your head or something, because we couldn't be more different,' Mo spluttered.

'That's not such a bad thing, bro. Look, I can see you're angry and I understand why, but we can't get the results we need if we don't take risks, you should know that by now. We've both been hurt, pretty much everyone on the team has, in some way or another, but we're still doing this because it's important. Surely you understand that?' Amir said.

'Of course I do, but that doesn't mean I have to accept it or like it, does it? Tell me again what your plan is.'

'I climb back into the storage room and set a fire, that's it,' Amir replied, missing out the part that if any other opportunities arose, he would likely take them.

'When are you planning on doing that?' Mo asked.

'Kendra and Trevor want to see where they go when they leave here, so first I have to go back and plant some GPS trackers. Once they leave and we can house them, I'll go back and start the fire, which should hopefully bring them all back here; while they're distracted, that's when Andy can clean them out.'

'Damn it, Amir, you can't keep putting yourself in so many spots, these guys have some serious weaponry!'

'Exactly my point, bro, we need to get the weapons back. My plan is for the fire to destroy the storeroom and therefore the documents they put there, so they won't miss what I stole. While they're trying to put the fire out, I believe that's when the military unit will go in and take them all out, so we can find the weapons.'

'I can shout and swear as much as I like, but it won't make a difference, will it?' Mo said, shrugging his shoulders in defeat.

'Sorry, bro, it needs to be done. I won't be long, I promise,' Amir said, patting his brother's arm affectionately before heading back towards the camper van.

Mo continued to shake his head as he watched his brother turn the corner.

'He makes it sound so bloody easy, but it never is,' he muttered.

Back in Marge, Amir gathered the extra kit he needed to carry out his plan, including a small bottle of petrol, some rags, matches, and a small fire extinguisher just in case; Kendra had insisted on the latter.

'Are the cameras live, Andy?' he asked. He had surprised them all by telling them he'd placed one camera inside the storage room and one on top of the door on the other side to cover the hallway. There was a small chance of it being spotted, although he'd placed it near the overhead door closer that ensured the fire door would close automatically if left open.

'Yes, all looking good. I've counted nine different Vietnamese men in the hallway so far, going into the first door on the right as you enter the hall from that end. I assume that's their main office. They've used a couple of other rooms, which are likely to be the kitchen and the toilet, so the remaining rooms must be storage rooms, also.'

'I guess the only thing we should worry about now is whether anyone stays here or whether they all leave,' Trevor said.

'That will be a problem, if they all leave, that's for sure,' Andy said.

'No problem, we won't set the fire if it's left empty, we can pivot to a home address instead if we need to.' Trevor hoped that it would be here, where they had little chance of being spotted.

'Just to be clear, I'll be setting the fire and then getting out quickly. When they start dealing with it, we wait until everyone is present before the military go in and take over?'

'That's the plan, but we all know that can change very quickly. I don't want it to be us taking them on, not with all those rifles,' Kendra said. 'Best leave it to those with experience in handling situations like this.'

'Okay, then I guess we wait and see what happens,' Amir said. 'I'm going in to sort out the GPS tags on the cars. They're all parked against the fence, so I should be able to reach through and attach them easily.'

'That reminds me, Rick messaged back to confirm that all three cars are registered to Legacy Solutions, much like we expected,' Kendra said, 'registered to the office in the flat they have just vacated, so not really of much help.'

'At least we know they all belong to Kam, so tagging them will be necessary,' Trevor said.

'Okay, well, I'm off now, see you later,' Amir said, waving.

'Just be careful, Amir, okay?' Kendra said, giving him a quick hug.

'Aren't I always?'

'No!' came the resounding reply from Kendra, Trevor and Andy.

AMIR TOOK the same route as before and followed the brook along its bank until he came to the fence. He'd brought half a dozen GPS tags, just in case, along with the glue he preferred to use and some duct tape, which was always handy. As ever, before doing anything, he took a minute to look and listen, and only made his move when he was confident the coast was clear.

First up was the silver Porsche Cayenne SUV. It was parked nose-in, so the tag would have to go at the front end, which wasn't ideal. Amir took a tag out of his pocket and added a dab of glue to each side before reaching through the bars of the fence and squeezing it behind the front number plate and its holder. It was a tight squeeze, but as the tag was coin-thin he was able to fit it in... just. The quick drying glue would keep it in place, no matter how rough the terrain.

Next was the silver BMW, which was parked rear-end against the fence. Amir repeated the process with the next tag then moved on to the third car, the black Mercedes, also parked with the rear end against the fence. Once he'd applied the glue, he slipped the tag between the rear bumper and the silver trim. Seconds later, he was moving back along the bank and away from the unit to safety. He called Kendra.

'All three GPS tags are in place, number zero-zero-eight for the Porsche, zero-zero-nine for the Mercedes, and zero-two-zero for the BMW, if you can let Andy know.'

'Thanks, Amir. Get yourself out of there and we'll call you when there's movement,' Kendra said.

'Hopefully that'll be soon, I need another adrenaline rush,' he teased.

'That's interesting,' Andy said, watching the monitor. 'Honestly, as much as I dread the stuff that he does, Amir doesn't half get results. If I'm not mistaken, that's two of our missing rifles coming out of the room next to the one he was in. That pretty much confirms the rifles are here.'

'I'll let the admiral know,' Trevor said, nodding in thanks. He dialled the number and sat on one of the narrow benches.

'Hello, Trevor, what's the update?' Sir Robert asked.

'We believe we've located the remaining rifles, sir. Two more have just surfaced from one of the rooms in the storage unit where we think they're being kept. That's five in the open and ten that are hidden, probably in that room.'

'Great news, thank you. How many people in the unit?'

'At the moment, we believe there are nine Vietnamese and five gang members. We believe some will be on the move soon, so I'm hoping our little distraction will have them all back here later where you can take them out,' Trevor replied.

'Is there any reason we can't do that sooner?'

'No, but by the time you get here, it's likely some will have left, so it's best you go in when they're all in situ.'

'Okay, I'll send a squad and have the team leader call you when they're in position,' the admiral said, 'and again, thank you for your efforts, Trevor, this is great work.'

'No problem, sir, I'll call when I have news.'

'All good?' Kendra asked.

'Yes, he's sending a squad to do the dirty work, so when we have all the players back here, we can send them in.'

'We have movement, people,' Andy said, 'the five gang members have just left and are heading for the Audi. All five are carrying what looks like an SA80 rifle, so wherever they're going, they mean business. All five rifles now in the back of the car, they are all into it, and the vehicle is off, off.'

'I'll call Mike and have the team get behind them,' Trevor said.

'Mike, we have the gang members on the move, all five in the Audi with a boot full of five SA80 rifles. They're heading away from the unit towards you.'

'Many thanks, Trevor, we'll take it from here.'

19

FIRE!

'The vehicle continues straight over into Southgate Road, continuing towards the M25, all units beware.'

The warning was a sign for all remaining surveillance units to get closer and prepare for the hazard that was the dreaded M25 motorway.

'It's the first exit, first exit onto the M25 eastbound, now a loss to eight-four, back-up over to you.'

'Five-five has vision, joins the main carriageway and continues M25 eastbound, speed increasing to seven-zero.'

'That's a relay, we're eastbound on the M25, all units close up,' Mike told his team.

They continued to follow the Audi for several junctions before turning southbound along the M11 towards London. After forty-five minutes, they approached the junction with the North Circular Road.

'Standby, standby, we're approaching the A406 junction, and it's a nearside indication at the split and now southbound along the A406.'

Mike updated Trevor.

'We're southbound on the A406 towards the A13, Trevor, there's a chance they could be heading back for another go at the hotel. Do you have a plan for that?'

'Not really, I mean the hotel is closed, there's nothing there at the moment except lots of police crime scene tape. Not sure what they'll be achieving, to be honest. Can you get anyone close in to see what they're up to?' Trevor asked.

'I'll send someone ahead while we're still on the A406, shouldn't be a problem. I'll call when I know more.'

'Thanks, Mike. You and your team are certainly earning your bonuses, aren't you?' Trevor laughed.

'Never joke about bonuses, Trevor, especially now we know what's at stake,' Mike said, hanging up and grinning to himself.

'Can I have a unit to get ahead to the hotel? We believe they're heading that way so it will be tricky for us to follow in the cars,' he asked.

'Six-three will do that.'

'Thank you, six-three. Eyeball, back to you.'

Shortly after acknowledging, six-three overtook the subjects' Audi and continued at speed ahead of them, heading for Khan's hotel.

As suspected, the Audi turned off towards the docklands, where just a few minutes later it headed towards the hotel.

'Six-three, it's a left, left and towards you. Now a loss to the eyeball.'

'All received by six-three. Contact, contact, subject vehicle now towards the car park. I can confirm there are no other vehicles or people here. It's a stop near the hotel. Five males have exited the

vehicle, four of them towards the rear as the fifth looks around. I can see rifles being handed to each male, including the look-out. That's confirmed, five rifles and they're on foot towards the hotel.'

'Six-three, is the hotel secured?' Mike asked.

'One-zero, that's confirmed. The entrances still have crime scene tape all over them. Standby, they're stopping short in a line and have started firing at the hotel. Blimey, I haven't seen that before, they're just spraying bullets all over it, there's glass falling from the broken windows. It's all a bit surreal,' six-three said. Mike called Trevor again.

'Trevor, they've turned up at the hotel and are just firing those weapons into it, smashing every window they can reach. What's the plan?'

'No idea, mate. I suppose we can get Rick involved, maybe do a hard stop or something. Let me call him and find out. In the meantime, stay out of range of those guns, you don't need me to tell you that, eh?'

'That's great advice, Trevor, I'll make sure to tell my team not to be heroes trying to block bullets!'

'Make sure you do!' Trevor said, laughing as he hung up.

'All units, they've stopped firing and are now back to the vehicle. The rifles are back in the boot and they're all into the Audi, which is now off, off and towards you. Now a loss to six-three.'

'Well, that was an interesting message they appear to be sending, of sorts,' Mike muttered as he joined the rear of the convoy, happy that his team were safe from gang members who didn't care a jot.

'THAT'S two of the cars now away, three in the Porsche and four in the Mercedes, with Kam being the driver of the

Porsche,' Andy told Trevor as he watched the monitor covering the storage unit car park. 'That leaves the BMW and two Vietnamese.'

'Thanks, Andy, that's a good sign they've left someone behind. I'm guessing the Audi will be back here in about thirty minutes or so with its gang reinforcements.'

'When do you want Amir to go back in?' Andy asked.

'The admiral messaged that his squad will be in the vicinity in the next twenty minutes, so I think we should wait until the Audi turns up and then call Amir in.'

'Sounds like a plan. I'll prep my computers to get into the four accounts and also to block Kam's phone and intercept the security checks from the banks, shouldn't take too long,' Andy said.

'That will be a nice healthy amount to steal from the bad guys, won't it?' Trevor said. 'We can do a lot of good with that.'

'Agreed, and bringing the surveillance team on board is a top move, Trevor; they will earn Sherwood Solutions a small fortune and expand our operation tremendously, especially the legitimate part of it.'

'Yeah, one of my better ideas,' Trevor said, patting Andy on the back, 'but let's not get ahead of ourselves just yet, there's still a lot to do, right?'

'Yes, there is. I'll monitor the Porsche and the Mercedes and see where they stop, it would be prudent to get an address or two before we take them out, right?'

'I'll leave it to you. K, you can stay here while I go and brief Amir. I want to make sure he does this next part exactly as he should,' he said, leaving the two together.

'I think he's warming to you, Mr Pike,' Kendra said, sitting next to Andy as he typed away.

'You think so? I guess it's better than a slap or a punch, he used to dish those out a lot!' Andy grimaced at the memories.

Kendra could see web pages changing rapidly on two separate monitors as Andy continued his preparations for the heist. She was deeply impressed by the skills she had never been privy to when they'd worked together. It was one of the things that had attracted her to him, the nerd he had hidden away so well, and now the dashing eye-patch-wearing computer genius who had helped the team accumulate millions from the criminals they had successfully taken on.

She also loved teasing him, playing on the deep emotions they had for each other, all in the hope they would one day rekindle the intimacy they'd come so close to enjoying. Smiling knowingly, she leaned over him as if to grab something on his other side, brushing against him provocatively. She felt him tense up and pause… just momentarily, before resuming the typing at his usual rapid pace. She grabbed a pen and repeated the slow brush as she brought it back with her.

'Sorry,' she whispered in his ear, 'I didn't mean to disturb you, Andy.'

He stopped typing and turned to look at her.

'You know very well that's exactly what you meant to do, Kendra. We've talked about this; we can't get involved while we're trying to save the world. You're not playing fair,' he chided.

Continuing to tease him, she fluttered her eyelashes.

'What's the matter, lover boy, can't handle a little flirting?'

Andy shook his head and turned back to his computer, determined not to show any emotion.

'Make yourself useful, Detective, and check the monitors behind you for any activity, will you?'

Kendra laughed and turned around to do as requested.

'I'm proud of you, Andy, you're becoming a worthy adversary,' she said.

'Adversary? Is that how you see me nowadays? Shame on you, and there's me thinking you're weak at the knees for me,' he said, smiling at the surprise on Kendra's face.

'Mr Pike, really?'

She punched him lightly in the arm and got up to leave.

'Check the damned monitors yourself,' she said, feigning anger.

'Oh, I don't need to, I've set up a sensor alarm, so I know exactly when something's happening.'

She flashed a smile and waved as she left.

When she'd gone, Andy blew a sigh of relief and paused for a few seconds.

Damn, that woman knows how to press my buttons.

'THE AUDI IS BACK, TREVOR,' Andy told him when he returned, 'and the Porsche and Mercedes have stopped in Southgate, a road called Cedar Rise, about twenty minutes away. They're parked on the driveway of number three, a large, detached house near the junction with Friars Walk. The house is registered to Legacy Solutions, before you ask, and it's worth a few quid, I can tell you.'

'Thanks, Mike just called to let me know his team has pulled off and is plotting around the roundabout, so we'll have someone here to follow anyone that gets away.'

'So, Amir can go back in?' Andy asked.

'He's already on the way, Kendra just gave him the green light. You'll see him pop up in a few minutes.'

'And so it begins,' Andy said theatrically as he turned to the monitor covering the storage unit.

'Are you ready to go with Kam's phone and bank accounts?' Trevor asked.

'Yes, it's all prepped, just need to know when to block the phone first, and the rest will be done within ten minutes or so.'

'Good man.'

'There's young Amir now,' Andy said as he watched the twin position himself in the CCTV blind spot again. After a short pause, he sprinted to the corner and immediately began to climb the drainpipe.

'Man, that boy can surely climb,' Trevor said, nodding in appreciation.

'I used to be a bit of a climber myself. You know, before I lost *this*,' Andy said, tapping his prosthetic foot with his ornate cane, which he always had close by. He smiled, waiting for some sympathy, or indeed *any* positive reaction from Kendra's father.

'Yeah, well, shit happens, doesn't it, Andy? You shouldn't have been messing around like you were, eh?' Trevor said, showing nothing of the sort.

'It was worth a try,' Andy muttered, turning back to see Amir going through the window and out of sight.

'Let's hope this doesn't take too long, he's been back in there way too many times, his luck is bound to run out soon,' Trevor said earnestly.

AMIR LISTENED at the door for any activity but could hear only murmured voices and the occasional laugh from downstairs, where he assumed the gang members would be. Content that it was clear, he took out the lighter fuel and rags from the plastic pouch he'd brought with him. He soaked two rags liberally and placed one on the bottom shelf where the nail salon products were, including the nail polish remover, acrylic gel and Isopropyl alcohol, all highly flammable. He took one of the bottles of alcohol and sprinkled it along the bottom shelf, before opening several bottles of the other flammable products.

The cunning intruder then went to the cabinets in the middle of the room and placed the soaked rag next to one of the documents boxes. He loosened all the lids to make sure the fire would do as much damage as possible, and also lay a few of the documents next to the rag to kickstart the flame. He examined his handiwork one last time before taking out a zippo lighter and lighting both rags. When he was happy they were both well-lit, he walked back to the window and began to make his exit. Before closing the window, he looked back and saw the flames spreading along the shelf. The documents on the cabinet had started to burn. He nodded happily.

'Time to go!'

'THERE GOES OUR SCRAPPY LITTLE FIRE-LIGHTER,' Andy said as he watched Amir make his typically graceful retreat.

'Look, you can see flames in the window, it won't be long now,' Kendra said, having joined the men in the camper van.

'It shouldn't be long before someone smells it, surely?' Trevor said.

'They'd better, because if they don't manage to put it out,

there's a chance they could lose the whole building,' Andy said.

'Ah, that would be a shame, wouldn't it?' Kendra smirked.

'Yeah, I'd like that too, but it would mess with the plan a bit, wouldn't it?' Trevor said.

'Aaand, there you go, the dread; the realisation that something is wrong,' Andy said as he saw activity on the first-floor hall.

They could see the two Vietnamese men pointing towards the storeroom, one of them then going into the kitchen and returning with a fire extinguisher. The gang members joined them on the hallway, two carrying extinguishers from downstairs, as they moved tentatively towards the door, from which wisps of smoke could be seen.

'Come on, chaps, leave it too long and you won't stand a chance of putting it out!' Andy said.

One of the gang members moved forward and quickly opened the door, before moving back quickly. One of his colleagues walked bravely into the smoke-ridden room and started spraying the extinguisher at the cabinets in front of him. The dry chemical extinguisher was the right one for the job and the fire was soon out, leaving a smouldering ruin. The other two men with extinguishers needed more time to put out the other fire, which was being fed by the flammable liquids on the lower shelf. Luckily for them, it hadn't spread too far for them to consider running for their lives. As with the fire on the cabinets, the damage was extensive.

The room was a stinking, smouldering ruin, covered with the white powder residue from the extinguishers. One of the Vietnamese men walked back into the hallway and made a call.

'Here we go, folks, Kam is receiving a call,' Andy announced.

They watched the monitor flicker as the call was happening, and Andy pointed to the other screen to confirm his current location hadn't changed.

'We should see some movement soon, I'm sure,' he added.

They watched as the Mercedes' GPS tag showed it on the move just a few minutes later. But not the Porsche.

'Damn it,' Trevor said, 'he's sending his goons but staying away. I was hoping they'd all be here.'

'We can grab him later, Dad, we have his phone tracked, and his car, there's no hiding place for him.'

They watched as the Mercedes drove towards Potters Bar. Trevor made some calls to Mike and the team to let them know what was going on, before calling Sir Robert.

'What's the update, Trevor?' the admiral asked.

'We currently have five gang members and two Vietnamese at the unit. There's one vehicle en route but we don't know how many occupants, I'd guess three or four. The main man is still in situ at an address twenty minutes away and we can track his movements if he does go anywhere.'

'The rifles?'

'As far as we can see, no more have been removed from the room, and the gang members have five in their possession, which they recently used to shoot up the hotel in Docklands.'

'Okay, my squad is ready, so when this other vehicle turns up, I'll send them in. I've given the team leader your number, so he'll call for you to identify the room where the rifles are. His call sign is Echo-three.'

'All received and understood, guvnor.'

'Please don't call me that, Trevor, you know how much I hate it when you do that.'

'Sorry, I'll revert to boss or sir, I can't be upsetting potentially our biggest client now, can I?' Trevor laughed.

'That's more like it. Give me a shout when you're ready.'

'Yes, guv, will do.'

Trevor laughed again and could only imagine Sir Robert shaking his head, before the admiral responded.

'You're an arse. Call me when you're ready.'

20

ECHO-THREE

The fire was completely out, and the room made safe by those in attendance by the time the Mercedes turned up. Four of Kam's henchmen from the car rushed upstairs to see the damage for themselves, including the two who usually dealt with the legal and accounting side.

'They don't seem happy, do they?' Kendra watched them gesture towards the sodden, plastic mess: all that was left of their precious documents.

'No, they don't, and the best thing is, they have no idea we have all the important deeds and documents needed to make some changes.' Andy grinned.

Trevor messaged Sir Robert to let him know that the Mercedes had arrived. Seconds later, his phone rang, *No Caller ID* displayed.

'This is Echo-three, I believe you've been expecting my call?'

'Yes. For your information, we now have a total of six Vietnamese and five gang members in the unit, five of the rifles are in their possession and to hand, the remainder we believe are hidden in a room on the first floor,' Trevor replied.

'Many thanks. My squad is now moving into position. We have two spotters to ensure we aren't disturbed, so tell your team not to make contact with anyone on the estate until we're clear.'

'Will do. Are you happy with the location of the unit, number five-delta?'

'Yes, yes, we'll just need some guidance within to find the weapons and also to give us a heads-up if anything goes wrong.'

'I'll be here when you need me,' Trevor responded.

'Received and understood,' the squad leader said before hanging up.

Trevor turned to Andy and Kendra.

'Get ready for the show; this should be very interesting indeed,' he told them, as all three turned towards the monitors.

'I'm guessing that's them?' A long-wheelbase Sky *Media* van had arrived close to the unit doors. The van's sliding door opened and six dark-clothed men wearing balaclavas and body armour, each carrying a rifle with a silencer, jumped out and ran towards the doors, which had been left unlocked by the Mercedes crew. Within a couple of seconds, they were all inside and out of view of the external monitor. The van with its single passenger drove away and parked close to the entrance, the armed occupants there to ensure their colleagues were not disturbed.

'Here we go,' Andy said, watching the feed from the internal camera on the first floor, where all six Vietnamese men were, along with three of the gang members. They were split between the storage room where the fire had occurred, where two gang members and one distraught Vietnamese man were carefully sifting through the remnants of the boxes. The third gang member was leaning against the wall in the hall near the door, watching as his friends were getting filthy. The remaining five Vietnamese men were in the meeting room, animatedly discussing the damage to their operation as a result of the fire. None of them heard the armed visitors take out the two gang members downstairs, who were handcuffed, hoods placed over their heads within the first ten seconds of entry, in complete silence.

Kendra, Andy and Trevor watched as the first two commandos appeared on the landing, rifles extended, as they moved along the hallway, quickly followed by two more, and then the final pair. The first pair, still unnoticed, entered the meeting room, much to the astonishment of the men inside.

'Armed police! Get down, now!' the first commando shouted.

They were joined by the second pair who also entered the room, shouting the same instruction to the stunned occupants.

Raheem, leader of the Deptford Mafia, who was enjoying watching Bethnal Green leader Imran and one of his men making a mess of themselves in the ruined room, heard the commotion and turned to see two armed men bearing down on him. Instinctively, he ran into the room and slammed the door shut.

'It's the police! Help me, now!' he shouted to his accomplices.

Imran and the other gang member quickly pushed two of the heavy cabinets against the door, as the banging started from the other side. The three of them then pushed against the cabinets as attempts were made to force the door open.

The Vietnamese lawyer, who was desperately looking for documents he could save, realised what was happening and took his phone out, dialling Raymond Kam.

'What is it, Tung?' Kam asked, his voice stern, matching his angry disposition.

'Sir, the police are here!' Tung shouted, the panic evident in his voice.

'What? The police? What the hell is going on there? Did you get away?' Kam asked, confused.

'I'm with three gangbangers, we've barricaded ourselves into the storeroom where the fire was.'

'Can you get to the rifles?' Kam asked.

'No, sir. What do you want me to do?'

'Listen to me. Say nothing, I will call our English lawyer to help you, Stevenson. Do you know what's happened to the others?'

'No, sir. It happened so quickly, the police must have them.'

'When you are taken to the police station, they must allow you a call. Call Stevenson and we will come and get you. Do you hear me?' Kam said.

'Y... yes sir,' Tung replied.

Kam ended the call, leaving Tung to stare at the door, which was now being smashed open by the armed men they all assumed were police. He withdrew into the corner and waited for them to enter and take them away.

He knew his time was up.

'KAM IS ON THE MOVE; his vehicle has just left and is moving at speed in this general direction,' Andy said, 'it's time for me to do some shipping.'

The first thing was to block Kam's phone, which took a couple of minutes. Andy correctly figured that Kam's attention would be centred on getting to Potters Bar to check on his men. There was a good chance he'd make calls along the way, but that he would be unlikely to be able to check while he was driving.

'Okay, his phone is now blocked, and I have the clone set up to intercept the bank authentication protocols,' Andy said as he continued to type, starting with the first bank account.

'This is going to be very satisfying,' he said.

RAHEEM, Imran and his accomplice realised they were about to be overwhelmed. Raheem had seen the Vietnamese man on the phone and realised he was informing Kam of the situation. The man was now in the corner, whimpering, knowing that his fate was out of his hands. He turned to Imran.

'How do you wanna do this, my friend?' he asked, smiling, his voice somewhat different than Imran had been used to.

'You mean whether we surrender, or we die? The rifles are downstairs, I don't know about you but all I have is a knife. Do we have a choice?'

'We always have a choice, Imran. This time, it's whether we wanna spend the next decade or more in prison, or not. I never wanna go back there, once was enough.'

'Stop talking madness, Raheem, we don't have a choice here. We put our hands up in the air like good boys and take our medicine, so we live to fight another day,' Imran said.

'You can do that if that's what you want. I might try something else.' Raheem stepped back from the cabinet he'd been pushing against the door. He walked back, quickly followed by Imran and the other gang member.

The door finally gave way, the cabinets screeching in protest as the armed intruders broke in.

'Armed police! Lie down on the floor, now!' one of them shouted.

Two more commandos joined him, and Raheem could see another in the hallway behind them, watching. He knew the odds were against him but could only think of the time he'd spent in the tiny cell at Pentonville prison. He smiled as he rushed the armed men, screaming at the top of his voice, his arms outstretched and ready to hurt the first man he made contact with. He failed.

He was dead before he hit the ground, the two shots to the chest from the expert marksman ensuring that Raheem's life ended in failure.

'Stupid, stupid man,' Imran whispered, shaking his head and lifting his arms higher.

'You two, down on the ground, now!' the shooter shouted.

They quickly did as ordered, where rough hands searched them, removing all their belongings. Imran saw them placed into a holdall.

The two gang members and the Vietnamese man lay there for several minutes as the armed men conducted their searches. One of them left the room to make two calls. One was to their colleagues outside in the van, requesting for the additional transport to be called in. The other, to Trevor.

'This is Echo-three. The unit is secured, one fatality, seven prisoners. Tell me where the rifles are.'

'As you leave the room where the fire was, it's the first room on the left. They should be in there somewhere,' Trevor replied.

'Many thanks,' Echo-three said.

'How will you be dealing with the fatality?' Trevor asked, hoping that the military would take care of it.

'We plan on leaving the body here so the local police can deal with it,' Echo-three said. 'After all, it won't take long for them to realise what's happened, right? The gang members' fingerprints are everywhere, along with those of the Vietnamese, so they'll put it down to a disagreement. Case closed, right?'

'You won't get any argument from me,' Trevor acknowledged.

'We'll take care of the foreign agents, but we may need you to take the gang members off our hands.'

'We can do that, but not now, you'll need to take them with you until we can take them off your hands later,' Trevor replied.

'Fair enough, we have another van en route to take them all away. I'll liaise with you later, Echo-three out.'

The squad leader sent two of his men to the room to search for the missing rifles. It took five minutes to find them, well-hidden underneath some foodstuffs. One of the men went back into the hall and gave the thumbs-up to Echo-three.

'How many?' the squad leader asked.

'Ten, Sarge.'

Echo-three nodded and returned the thumbs-up.

'Get them downstairs and ready to ship out, along with the prisoners,' he ordered.

Apart from the shooting, the mission was a success, achieving its objectives and taking a number of very nasty people off the streets of London... permanently.

Andy had made swift progress.

The first transfer to a crypto wallet took just a minute. While waiting for the security procedure to kick in, he continued to another bank account and did the same, and then to the third and fourth accounts. The clone phone pinged four times, one after the other, with the two-factor authentication codes that each bank required to continue with the transfers. Andy obliged on each occasion, with the transfers all going ahead thanks to the additional security measures he'd checked and disabled, including limits on transfers. The entire process took less than the ten minutes he'd estimated, such was the speed he worked at. Kendra marvelled that he was able to do so much in such a short amount of time.

'How do you know all this stuff again?' she asked.

'Lots and lots of practice makes perfect, remember? Doing it is pretty straightforward when you can pretend to be the account holder, it's doing it quickly enough to clear the accounts and transfer the funds before the owner finds out, that's the skill. I guess I'm a natural,' he said with a grin.

'Bravo, that's all I can say,' Kendra said, nodding in appreciation.

'Aaand, done!' he replied, exaggerating the last press of a key. 'The transfers are done, I now need to unblock his phone and then transfer the funds from the crypto account to one of our overseas banks, and then I can repeat the process from that account to another, making it impossible to trace.'

Having unblocked Kam's phone, he then proceeded to do as he'd explained to Kendra, transferring the crypto funds to one of their Cayman Island accounts. Once complete, he then transferred those same funds back into another crypto wallet and repeated the process by transferring to their other account.

'How much did you grab, Andy?' Trevor asked, bemused by the ease in which Andy dealt with the theft.

'After the crypto and bank fees and factoring currency exchange fees, the final amount in our Sherwood Management Trust and the Loxley Investments accounts amounts to... eighteen million, two hundred and fifteen thousand pounds and some loose change,' he said, giggling as he saw Trevor's mouth drop.

'That's a lot of money,' Kendra said. 'Well done, that man,' she added, rubbing his shoulder affectionately.

'Yes, it is, which I'm sure we'll put to good use as we always have done, right?'

'Some of it will go back to the victims of these bastards,' said Trevor, 'we just need to figure out how we're going to find them. Also, we have to change ownership on the properties they stole from people, which may be easier as the records are pretty good.'

'I've already started on that,' said Andy. 'I've made a bunch of changes with Land Registry; the process takes a while, but Kam won't have a clue that all the properties are being transferred to their previous owners. That may upset him a little.'

'Won't he just go after them again?' Kendra asked.

'Exactly, which is why we need to get him off the streets,' Trevor said. 'By last count, it's him and two others still on the loose, right?'

'Here in London, yes, but there are likely to be more of them around the country, surely?' Kendra said.

'If we can get hold of one of their computers from the

unit, I can collate all his people and we can decide on how best to deal with them later,' Andy said.

'I'll call Echo-three.' Trevor made the call.

'What can I do for you?' came the reply.

'Can you grab one of their laptops on the way out? One that isn't locked with a password, preferably,' he asked.

'Will do, you can send one of your people down to pick it up in about five minutes, as we're leaving.'

Mike Romain took Trevor's call and volunteered to pick the laptop up himself.

'Thanks, Mike. Hopefully that will be the worst of it out of the way, just three of them left, including the boss.'

'Like you said, the vehicle is tracked, so it's only a matter of time.'

'Speak of the devil, he's due to arrive here in about five minutes, by which time I hope everyone is away from there. Can you get it picked up now?' Trevor asked.

'I'm on my way there now, so I should be in and out in a couple of minutes,' said Mike.

'Phew, there's a lot of organising going on with this job, that's for sure,' Trevor said, wiping his brow theatrically.

'All in a good day's work, Dad, remember that!' Kendra laughed.

21

DISCOVERY

The back-up transport arrived, another long-wheelbase van, plenty of space and anonymous. The armed squad took the prisoners out one at a time to limit exposure, loading them into the back and securing them to the benches that ran along each side and behind the cabin.

Mike Romain arrived as they were loading the last of the prisoners.

Just as Mike got back into the car, the message came out over his radio.

'Standby, standby, vehicle one is approaching the roundabout, all units beware.'

Mike calmly drove away, looking into his rearview mirror to see if the armed unit had received the same message.

They had.

The movement behind him was calm but energised as the armed squad all jumped into the rear of the *Sky Media* van, which was then driven away from the unit, leaving the van that was transporting the prisoners for its driver to secure it and leave. The sliding door was slammed shut and the driver climbed in and acknowledged the plain-clothed passenger who had accompanied him to the estate. He drove away from the unit as Kam and his two men approached in the Porsche.

Kam had seen movement from the distance and realised, when he saw the two vans pass him, neither of them police vehicles, that something had gone badly wrong, his instincts giving him an ache in his stomach that he hadn't felt since the family had escaped US law enforcement many years earlier. The occupants of the vans were anonymous-looking and did not make eye contact with him as they passed, indicating that they were professionals. As he pulled up to the storage unit, there was nothing to suggest anything had gone wrong. It was only when they entered that it was evident something had.

Kam could smell the smoke from the earlier fire and could see from the mess on the ground floor that there had been much activity, albeit with no sign of blood or bodies. Upstairs was a different story. The meeting room had been ransacked and chairs were left strewn on the floor, amongst other debris including laptops, printers, and documents.

One of his men had gone straight to the room where the weapons had been stored. It wasn't long before he returned.

'Sir, they're gone... all of them,' he said.

Kam nodded, expecting nothing less. The man left to check the storeroom and very soon called back to his boss to join him. The man pointed when Kam entered the room. He was pointing to a body on the floor. A dead body.

Kam nodded again, recognising Raheem but happy that it wasn't one of his own, until he realised the rest of his men were nowhere to be seen. Six of them, including his lawyer and accountant... gone. He realised that the damage to his organisation could be severe. Although he trusted his men not to say anything, knowing of the potential threats to their families, Kam knew the UK police were proficient and would eventually find evidence of wrongdoing within the organisation. He had no clue that it wasn't the police that were responsible.

'Get the computers, quickly, we must leave!' he ordered.

His men obliged and retrieved three laptops before they left, leaving the dead body behind.

The police will point the finger at us, of this I am sure, he thought. It was time to leave the London operation behind and regroup.

MIKE CALLED Trevor to update him.

'The Porsche is away. We left just in time, by the skin of our teeth!'

'That's how the best of the best work, Mike, it's all about small margins. Just to catch you up, there was one fatality, one of the gang members, and all the rifles were accounted for, so a job well done by all.'

'Good, so, hopefully, once we get the boss, it'll put the organisation out of business,' Mike said.

'We've made some progress with that, but it's important to finish this before Kam finds out what we're doing and tries to put a stop to it, including taking revenge.'

'Understood. I'll wait for your instructions.'

Trevor turned to Kendra and Mike.

'That was a hectic hour or two, wasn't it?' he said, exhaling as he sat down.

Andy continued to type, making sure everything he'd said he was going to do was done and then checked over.

'What now, Dad? I'm guessing we wait until Kam goes home, isn't that going to make it difficult to take him out?' Kendra asked.

'Probably, but I thought we could get Rick involved; it's time to give him some more overtime, don't you think?'

'Hmm, I'm sure Aileen will be pleased,' she said, referring to Rick's wife.

'I'm kidding,' said Trevor, this is just a natural progression of their case, isn't it? If we get him involved, he can use his police contacts to locate the rest of Kam's organisation countrywide and put an end to them, once and for all.'

'Hopefully I can give them a heads-up when Mike gets me the laptops,' said Andy, 'I'm sure they'll have some very useful contact information on there, although I think Google Translate may be a lifesaver.'

'Okay, I'll call Rick and update him now. I may have to go into work tomorrow to start helping out, I've been absent way too long,' Kendra said.

'Okay, love, go and call him and let me know if he needs anything else from us.'

Kendra left the van to call Rick, leaving Trevor alone with Andy.

'So, eighteen million pounds, eh? What do you reckon? Think we should start enjoying the fruits of our labour?' Trevor asked, trying to gauge Andy's reaction.

It didn't work.

'Trevor, you should know me by now, and you should know better than that. Money means very little to me, haven't I been clear about that? I have millions of my own stashed away, but I live in a modest terraced house and drive around in a camper van. I have everything in life I need and I'm not greedy, so don't worry about me being a wrong 'un, because I'm not.'

Trevor nodded respectfully, seeing how serious Andy was with his response. He had noticed Kendra and Andy getting closer recently, forgetting their agreement and acting naturally, and he felt guilty for them both.

'Sorry, Andy, I meant nothing bad. I just want the best for you and my daughter, and I see that it's difficult for you. I thought you'd see this money as an opportunity to quit and offer her a decent life.'

Andy laughed.

'Seriously? Do you know what would happen if I went to her and said... "Kendra, how about I take you away from all this, we have all the money we need and can have a great life travelling the world"? I tell you what would happen, she'd poke me in my good eye and stomp on my remaining foot, and then not talk to me for weeks!'

Trevor laughed at the image of Andy hopping between his prosthetic foot and his good foot, his arms out and unable to see, but again nodded respectfully.

'You know my daughter better than I ever realised, mate, I stand corrected and rebuked,' he said, bowing theatrically.

'That's good, because she's much better than either of us realise, Trevor, and she deserves everything in life that she wants.'

He turned away, saddened by the thought that he might not be a part of that.

Andy and Kendra had agreed they wouldn't get involved in a relationship due to the dangers involved. Dealing with unpredictable criminals outside of the law was never going to be easy, so he understood their reluctance to get involved while there was a chance they could be used as pawns against each other and against the team.

'You know, I've been thinking about your pact with Kendra.'

'What do you mean? You know we're not doing anything, right? Honest, I'm not trying to pull a fast one,' Andy said, raising his arms in surrender.

Trevor laughed.

'I know, I know, so calm down. What I mean to say is that you made that pact when we were a relatively small and inexperienced team, when the dangers were very real and very frequent. I get that, I understood it, and I supported it. But things have changed.'

'I'm not following you.'

'Andy, we've made great strides these last couple of years. The team has grown, we've become very good at what we do. More to the point, we know how to protect each other and we have the team and the technology to do that much better than when you made your pact.'

'What are you saying, Trevor? That me and Kendra should... date?' Andy got out of his seat and stepped back a couple of paces.

Trevor laughed again.

'Come on, when was the last time I slapped you? We're cool, sit back down.'

'Okay, but first, tell me what you meant, because what I heard was that times have changed, and you think our pact is out of date?'

'Yes, I do. I think you two should sit down and realise that unless you give it a go you could regret it later. For example, what if something *did* happen to one of you? How would you feel, if you'd never given your feelings a chance to blossom? You could very easily spend the rest of your life regretting it.'

'Wait, so you are okay with my dating Kendra?'

'Andy, we've had our disagreements, for sure. I may not have approved of... well, a lot of what you do. But, and I have to give you credit for this, most of your decisions have been spot on and have made this team better. I have to give you major credit for that. But most of all, I know how you feel about my daughter; I see it in your eyes, your protective nature when it comes to her, everything about you screams of your love for her. Of course I approve.'

Andy was stunned and sat back down, heavily, staring at Trevor as if expecting him to point a finger and say *only joking, fool!*

'You know, it's one of those moments, I think.' Trevor laughed again.

'What's that?' Andy asked.

'If I had a microphone, I'd drop it,' he said, miming a mic drop and climbing out of the camper van.

KAM ARRIVED BACK at the house in Southgate and ordered his men to pack.

'We must leave London until things calm down. Too much has happened, and they will be pointing fingers at us for that idiot's death,' he told his men. 'We must regroup and find new lawyers who can protect us before we come back. Take only essentials, we will return here one day soon.'

His men did as they were ordered. Kam went to his room and lifted the carpet in one corner of the small, walk-in wardrobe to reveal a small safe. He opened the safe and checked the contents. There were eight bundles of fifty-pound notes, totalling twenty thousand pounds, four credit cards with high limits, two burner phones, and a Heckler and Koch SFP9 handgun with two spare clips. He also had two passports, one Vietnamese and one American, both in fake names but both skilful forgeries that would get him out of the country if needed. He nodded, knowing he had what he needed if he had to move fast.

He was expecting things to get worse before they got better, so it was prudent to plan an exit strategy. He took out his phone and logged into his primary bank account app so that he could stop off and pick up more cash on the way out of London. The app, as expected, requested two-factor authentication to confirm the account holder, and Kam entered the six-digit code when it was sent to his phone.

'This cannot be right,' he whispered, as he saw the account balance. He logged out and logged in again, again after the two-factor authentication was confirmed. The balance was the same. Zero.

Kam logged out and furiously started to log into one of the secondary accounts, fearing the worst. Those fears were confirmed: all four accounts were empty.

His men heard his screams and knew the journey out of this accursed city would be a long and painful one.

22

MEETING

'What are you grinning at?' Kendra asked when she entered the camper van.

'Kam has just found out that he has no money left.' Andy smirked. 'He received five different codes from the banks, which means he's now definitely aware that he's skint. He won't be a happy man. He'll be an angry man, a very angry man.'

'That's good—and wait till he finds out he has no properties left, either,' Kendra said.

'That one may be a bit trickier, he still has time to interrupt the process I started, to transfer everything. That's why we need to keep him busy.'

'Dad is on his way over; I just spoke to Rick but will wait until you're both here to give you the update.'

'Did you give him the associate names and information for the rest of Kam's organisation?' Andy asked, having retrieved it from the laptops.

'Yes, it will help a lot. It will also keep him and the team busy for a while. I'll pop in tomorrow and help out,' she said.

'Listen, can we have a chat later? Just the two of us? There's something I need to talk to you about,' Andy said, slightly nervous but feeling braver than he had in a long time, thanks to Trevor.

'Sure. Anything I should be worried about?'

'Well, to be honest, yes.' He smiled knowingly as Trevor walked in.

'Perfect timing, as ever, Trevor,' he said, turning back to Kendra to see confusion on her face.

'Really, why's that?' Trevor asked.

'Kendra has a major update for us,' he said. 'Over to you, Detective.'

'Why, thank you, Mr Pike,' she said, bowing.

Trevor shook his head. 'You two are like peas in a pod, honestly.'

'I'll take that as a compliment, Father,' Kendra said, grinning. 'Anyway, on to more pressing things. I spoke with Rick, and they are progressing well with the evidence relating to the hotel attack and will be charging the gang members they have in custody. Some of them have turned on each other, which is damning and will lead to hefty prison terms.'

'We hope,' Andy added.

'Additionally, I have passed on to Rick the anonymous information relating to the Vietnamese gang and their nationwide operations. He has instigated some investigations in Birmingham, Liverpool, Manchester, Newcastle, and Edinburgh. It mainly relates to the use of illegal immigrants being used as cheap labour in exchange for accommodation and food at the businesses the Vietnamese have taken over. He reckons they'll be raiding the businesses in the next two days.'

'Where does that leave the properties that we're trying to change ownership on? Won't it affect that?' Andy asked.

'It may do, but the priority here is to take everything away from Kam so he isn't able to function again in this country,' Kendra replied.

'Even if he gets away, which is unlikely,' Trevor added.

'That's right. As we speak, there's four of them that we know of, including Kam, in this part of the world. Rick's contacts should be able to take care of the rest of the organisation.'

'It's important that they stop all their businesses, otherwise they'll just keep generating more money, which will allow them to restart if he gets away,' Andy said, 'so hopefully those raids go ahead as soon as possible.'

'Rick is aware and is briefing his contacts regularly, so I'm sure everything will be done. They'll be working with the Home Office, who will want to take the migrants into custody. Many of them will claim asylum to try to stay in the country but it won't take long to figure out who the genuine claimants are. The main thing is that the businesses will be closed with immediate effect,' Kendra said.

'So, what's our next step?' Trevor asked.

'We need to move quickly on Kam before he has a chance to figure out what we're doing with the properties. I know we took a lot of money from him, but the properties he has ownership of are worth even more than the eighteen million we've taken; there are hotels and shop premises as well as expensive houses. If he retains those, he'll be able to sell and start again, so we need to distract him enough for him not to check,' Andy said.

'Okay, any ideas how?' Kendra asked.

'We need to take them off the streets,' Andy said. 'I suggest a nice simple trap for him to fall into.'

'Go on,' Trevor said.

Andy picked up one of the burner phones and showed it to them.

'This is a clone of his phone, remember? I can send a message from another phone telling him that we have his money and if he wants to see it again, he needs to meet with us.'

'What makes you think he'll fall for that?' Kendra asked. 'It sounds too simple, if you ask me.'

'That's the beauty of it, we want him to expect a trap. What you forget is that we also have a tracker on his phone and his car. With the cloned phone, we'll know every move he makes and everything he does to counter our trap, and then deal with him on our terms.'

Kendra looked at Trevor.

'Sounds feasible, but you often say that things are always likely to go wrong. What do you think, Dad?'

'First off, I think Andy is right and that we need to deal with Kam quickly. Getting the properties is critical for our plan to work and put them out of business for good. The trap may not work, though, because we only have tracking on Kam and his car, not his accomplices. He'll likely send them off to do his bidding and we won't have a clue what they get up to.'

'That's where your mate Mike Romain comes in. You say he's the best; well, if you get his team in position, they can follow Kam's men and see what they get up to,' Andy said.

'That works for me,' Trevor said, taking out his phone.

'How goes it, Trev?' Mike asked. 'The team are scattered in the Southgate area; I assume Kam hasn't moved yet?'

'No, but he will do very soon. I'm about to put a call in to lure him out. Here's the thing, I need you to follow his men only; not Kam, just his men. We're setting a trap for Kam, and we need to know where he sends his men and what they're likely to get up to. Can you do that?'

'Sure. It will mean sending a footie in to cover the house and then potentially splitting the team up if the accomplices split. Yeah, we can do that.'

'Great. Get them in position now and expect movement soon.'

'On it now,' Mike said, hanging up.

Trevor turned to Andy. 'Your turn, make the call.'

Andy picked up a different burner phone and dialled Kam's number.

'Who is this?' Kam replied warily.

'This is your friendly babysitter,' Andy said, 'we're babysitting your money, Mr Kam.'

There were several seconds of silence.

'Why are you calling me? To gloat?'

'No, not at all,' Andy said, 'I'm calling to make a business proposition, that's all. If it works out, you get your money back and we're all happy.'

'Why will you be happy? What do you want?'

'We want you to leave the London hotels alone for us, all of them. You can have the rest of the country, but London is out of bounds.'

Kam again took a few seconds to digest the words, sensing hope in getting the money back.

'I am listening.'

'We will meet and discuss in person. If you agree to our terms, you will sign a document that precludes you and your company, including future companies, from doing business in the greater London area. If you sign, we will transfer the funds back to you there and then,' Andy said. 'If you don't, you will never see that money again and we will go to war with you in London. It is your choice, Mr Kam.'

'Where and when?' Kam asked.

'Jubilee Park in Edmonton. We will meet you there; as you go in through the Galliard Road entrance, there is a path on the left that leads to some benches around a circular display. Be there in two hours, no weapons, alone, and I will do the same,' Andy said, pointing to a map on one of the monitors for Trevor and Kendra to see.

'Two hours, I will be there,' Kam said, and hung up. He called to his remaining men, who joined him in the spacious lounge.

'They called and want to meet me in a park. I want you to go there now and see where you can hide and take them out when I get our money back. It is a trap, of that I am sure, so go now, quickly, and be careful as they may be doing the same there.'

'Which park, boss?'

'Jubilee Park in Edmonton, maybe fifteen minutes away. Go now and call me when you get there.' Kam handed a set of car keys to one of the men. 'Take the Jaguar. I'll come in my car when you call and confirm that all is well.'

He watched as the three men departed in haste.

Someone will die for this, he thought, clenching his fists.

'CONTACT, *contact to nine-two, three men out, out of the front door and to the garage, which is opening. All three men towards a silver*

Jaguar, hotel-Juliet-seven-zero-echo-Romeo, uniform. Stand by for movement,' said Lynn, now on foot, as she warned her colleagues over the radio.

The message was quickly relayed.

'The vehicle is reversing off the drive and now off, off towards Friar's walk and a right, right. Loss to nine-two.'

'All units let's give them a loose follow, there is a tracker on the car so low risk. I need one unit to go ahead at speed and be in position at Jubilee Park before they arrive,' Mike requested.

Mike called Trevor to update him.

'They're on the move, Trevor. They're using a white Jag, three up, which is handy, and I've sent a unit ahead to get into position for their arrival.'

'Thanks, Mike. Tell your people to be careful, these guys are nasty and most likely armed.'

'Will do. What's the plan when they get here?'

'We're thinking of maybe disabling the car and securing them when they return to it, just need to figure out a way of doing that without anyone getting hurt,' Trevor replied.

'Can your friends in the military come and get them?'

'I doubt it. The location is quite open there, with lots of residential housing where they're likely to park. I'm calling Rick to see if he has anyone in mind,' Trevor replied.

'Okay, they'll need to move fast, I reckon we will be there in about fifteen minutes.'

'Calling now,' Trevor said, ending the call. He called Rick immediately.

'Can you get an armed unit to secure three armed men in a park?' he asked.

'When do you need them for?' Rick asked.

'I'd say about an hour and a half. They're on the way to a

park in Edmonton, north London, where they'll be hiding for that time waiting for a meeting between Kam and a fictious person. We're keeping him distracted as long as we can, to stop him from finding out about the properties. He's alone in the house now, and has his car, but we're not sure when or if he's going to make it to the meeting itself. We want these men taken out before he gets here, preferably.'

'Will you be able to pinpoint their location to the armed officers?' Rick asked, 'and is there a likelihood of a firefight?'

'I'm going to say yes and yes.'

'Is there any way to prevent any shooting?'

'I can't say, Rick. I don't want any of our people getting close, for obvious reasons, and I don't want any connections made to us. Got any ideas?'

'Ideally, if we can get them all in the car, the armed units can take them out without too much difficulty,' Rick replied.

'Let me have a think. In the meantime, if you can put something in motion on your end, I'll call you back when I know more.'

Trevor ended the call and rang Andy.

'Andy, just spoke to Rick and he has concerns about an armed unit taking the bad guys out in the park. Is there a way we can get them back in the car when they arrive and do their recon?'

'I can call and reschedule or cancel the meet, I suppose?' Andy replied.

'How about disabling the vehicle itself, somewhere quiet. Can you do that?'

'I don't think so. These modern cars have pretty good security, I'll check, but I'm not sure. How much time do we have?'

'Let's say an hour or so?'

'Okay, I'll call back soon.'

'It's starting to get hectic again, isn't it?' Kendra said.

Trevor smiled and nodded reassuringly. 'All in a day's work, love.'

ANDY KNEW it would be tricky to take control of the Jaguar, such was its high level of security. He had one hope only, that someone on the dark web was in the know, was online at this time, and was willing to assist him. He signed on via the Hades program and entered one of the community chat rooms that he knew were frequented by the person he was looking for.

'Okay, guys and gals, I need to know how to hack into a modern Jaguar, if it is possible. Any takers? Some lovely shiny bitcoin on offer if anyone comes through,' he typed.

He waited patiently for a response, knowing full well that the occupants of the room were all there for one reason only, to earn untraceable crypto currency that hackers now favoured above anything else.

'Do you have access to the car?' asked one.

'No,' Andy replied.

'Bluetooth?' asked another.

'Yes, but I don't have any devices paired to it,' Andy answered.

'Can you break into it?'

'Doubtful, it will likely be parked on a public street.'

'I can get you in,' a third person answered, call sign *Turniphead89*.

'If you can get into this vehicle then message me privately and

we can discuss,' Andy replied, *'I have an urgent deadline, so no timewasters please.'*

Andy saw that *Turniphead89* had left the chat room. Seconds later, he received a private message from them.

'Like I said, I can get you in.'

'How?' Andy asked.

'What are you paying?'

'Nought-point-one,' Andy replied, 'which is about five thousand three hundred British pounds.'

'That's not a bad offer, but this is a very useful bit of software, so make it nought-point-two and you have a deal,' the hacker countered, doubling the amount.

'That's a lot of money for something I don't know works, but I need it quick, so you have a deal. How do we do this?'

'Half up front and half after you get in.'

'Okay, send me your wallet details and I'll make the payment now. I need the info immediately.'

'Just one thing, you'll need a smart phone and a car fob, any regular car fob.'

'Not a problem.'

'Sending you my crypto wallet now.'

Andy saw the lengthy account number come through.

'Sending half the payment now,' Andy typed, before copying the wallet number and transferring the bitcoin to it.

'Got it, thanks. So, download the link I'm sending you now onto the phone that will be used. It basically acts like a portable router but with a tweak that allows it to mirror the signals that emanate from the car when the driver uses their key fob to get in,' the hacker explained.

'So how will it work with a fob from a different car?' Andy asked.

'The signal the wrong fob sends will be met with the car's own

signal, which checks and verifies it. Normally, it will reject it as the wrong key, quite correctly, but my program changes the fob signal via the phone to mirror the one used to check it, so it will open the car. Once you're in, you can then use the phone to disrupt the electrics using the bespoke control interface that I created. It can't make the brakes fail or do any of that TV stuff, but it can mess with electrics and make it go into limp mode, keep the windows and doors locked, and change the air conditioning temperature, that sort of thing.'

'Bloody hell, how many people know of this?'

'Not that many. I usually charge a lot more, but you have quite a reputation on here, so I want to keep on your good side,' the hacker replied, adding a smiley emoji.

'That's good of you, I appreciate it,' Andy said. 'Any last-minute instructions?'

'Not really, just that whoever uses it needs to be close, probably within thirty feet, otherwise the signal may be too weak.'

'You're a star, thank you. I'll be in touch soon,' Andy replied, signing out of the Hades program.

'What now?' Trevor asked.

'I need to send a link to one of the surveillance team so they can get access to the car and mess with it. Can you get in touch with Mike?'

'This is going to be so much fun,' Trevor said. 'I'll let Rick know what's going on, too, he should know what is about to happen.'

MIKE ACKNOWLEDGED Trevor's instructions and assigned Lynn the task of getting close to the white Jaguar. He sent her the link and explained the process, asking her to learn it quickly as the vehicle would be arriving at the plot very soon.

'All units, we're approaching the park. Eight-four, are you in position?' Mike asked.

'Yes, yes, in position. The park is almost empty and there is nobody close to the location given for the meet.'

'Good. When the targets leave the vehicle, we will attempt to gain access to it and keep them in it while we wait for the firearms units, for all your info,' Mike said. *'Eyeball, back to you.'*

'Standby, we have brake lights, and it's an offside indication towards the park entrance. It will be a loss to me shortly, back-up can you take?'

'Yes, yes, five-five has the eye. It's a stop, stop in the car park. I have good vision on the vehicle, units hold back or take alternatives,' the surveillance officer said, *'All three men are out, out of the vehicle and into the park. It's a loss to me on the men but I'll maintain my position for the vehicle, five-five over.'*

'Contact, contact to eight-four. The three men are heading nearside towards the meeting point, looking around. I can confirm: nobody else in the vicinity at this time. They're splitting up and taking separate paths towards the circular display. Stand by.'

'Barry, what is their body language saying?' Mike asked.

'They've met up at the display and are chatting, looking around and pointing in different directions. They're looking for places to hide, I think. Eight-four, over.'

'Got it, thanks. Let me know when they've settled so I can send Lynn to the car,' Mike said.

'Okay, we have movement. One of the men is on the phone and all three are now walking away from the display in different directions.'

'Barry, any risk to you?' Mike asked.

'Negative, I have good cover. Okay, one is now hiding by a

storage shed, which is straight ahead as you come into the park, twelve o'clock. Another is hiding in a clump of trees and bushes at ten o'clock and the third is at six o'clock, close to the entrance behind some bushes. They're pretty well hidden and can be at the display in less than ten seconds.'

'All received. Lynn, that's your cue,' Mike said.

'Moving towards the car now,' Lynn replied.

This is where things could start to go wrong, Mike thought.

23

ARMED RESPONSE

Lynn was one of the more experienced surveillance officers, having worked as an operative on several of the elite Counter Terrorism Command surveillance teams in the Metropolitan Police, following terror subjects for many years. The thrill of the follow made her miss it terribly when she retired, and it didn't take long for her to consider Mike Romain's offer to join his private sector team. The fact that it paid very well was a fabulous bonus, and working on operations such as this made her a very happy person indeed.

Nobody would think her out of place if they saw her walking down the street. She had changed into a dark-green jacket to go with her blue jeans and black trainers and had tied her brown hair into a ponytail. She walked with purpose, constantly scanning the immediate vicinity and beyond for any potential threats or hazards. She could see the white Jaguar parked in the small car park by the entrance, with another four cars alongside it.

The main entrance had a beautiful semi-circular iron

gate. The large central gates were closed, occasionally opened only for vehicular access. There were two pedestrian entrances on either side, with much smaller gates. Running next to the pavement were low, metal, ornamental fence, acting as the divide between the car park and the pavement. Lynn could see no other option but to stay close to the vehicle and try to look as normal as possible. She sat on the low fence and spoke into her covert microphone.

'Eyeball, permission.'

'Go ahead.'

'Nine-two in position but it isn't ideal, for your info,' she said.

'All received, Lynn. Do what you need to do, and eight-four will give you a heads-up if you're likely to be interrupted,' Mike replied.

After having another look around for potential hazards, Lynn took the phone out that she had downloaded the software onto and turned it on. She opened the app and started the process of initiating the software that would give them access to the vehicle. As soon as the app was ready, she took out her car keys and covertly aimed the fob towards the Jaguar. She first pressed the start button for the software to activate and then, two seconds later, pressed the fob, ready to make a quick exit if it went wrong.

It took ten seconds for something to happen, and when it did, it took her by surprise. The hazard lights on the Jaguar flashed once and she heard the doors unlock. She was so surprised that she looked around guiltily, as if she'd been caught in the act by a passer-by, breathing a sigh of relief when she realised that she was still alone.

Is that it? she thought, looking down at the app. Knowing that the control radius was only thirty feet, she activated limp mode, so if the car was to drive off it would be severely restricted in speed and performance. She also locked the windows so the occupants wouldn't be able to open them, and then turned the air conditioning on at full heat. She could hear the fans blowing from where she sat and smiled to herself as she tried to imagine what the men would think when they got back inside. It would also drain the battery, which would be a bonus.

'Access gained, there's not much else I can do here, do you want me to stay in position, one-zero?'

'Yes, yes, until the armed units are in place, and then you can discreetly leave it to them,' Mike replied.

Once he knew the car was primed, he called Trevor.

'That's a hell of a bit of kit there, Trev, can we keep it?'

'I'm sure we can, Andy's the man to ask. Did it work okay?'

'It did, yes. I've left a unit on foot close to the car until I know the firearms units are close by. I don't want my people involved, so can you find out what the ETA is?'

'I'll call Rick now and find out,' Trevor replied. 'The car has been accessed so that when the men are back in it and the firearms unit is in position, they can take it out wherever they feel comfortable,' he told Rick.

'Excellent. Where are the targets now?'

'They're hiding in some bushes in the park waiting for the opposition to turn up, but they'll be getting a call to return to Kam when he's told the meeting is off. We'll put that call in when the firearms unit is in position.'

'Okay, I'll call them now, I imagine they'll be there very soon,' Rick said.

He called Trevor back less than five minutes later. 'They'll be on the plot in six minutes.'

'Great; thanks, Rick. I'll send you Mike's number so that

you can liaise with him directly for real-time movement. Please ensure to keep his team out of it; only the firearms unit can deal with it based on an anonymous tip-off.'

'Understood, and don't worry, I've got that lie down to a tee.'

KAM TOOK the call from one of his lieutenants.

'How does it look there?' he asked.

'It is quiet, sir, but we will see anyone arriving and can deal with them quickly if needed.'

'You will do nothing until I tell you, do you understand?' Kam shouted, 'If this is a legitimate meeting and you jeopardise it, I will rip your ears from your head, do you hear me?'

'Yes, sir!'

'I will make my way there and aim to be there at the appointed time. I will only show myself if you are sure that it is not a trap, otherwise I will make my way back to the house.'

'Understood, sir.'

Kam ended the call, the feeling of unease still with him.. He looked at his watch, intending to leave in thirty minutes unless he heard anything negative from his men. Everything that he'd worked so hard for over the past years was at risk. With everything he had in place outside of London, he could still run a lucrative operation, despite losing the eighteen million, and it wouldn't take long to recoup that, but he had to take measures to prevent it ever happening again.

Sensing the seriousness of the situation, he went to the safe that he'd checked earlier, hidden in the floor of the walk-in wardrobe. He removed the handgun and two spare clips, the burner phones, the passports, and the twenty thousand pounds, placing everything from the safe into a backpack. He went back downstairs and put his laptop in the same bag along with its charger and a flash drive that he'd copied everything onto.

The nagging feeling was still there so his mind was made up: to plan as if he were on the run from the police. *'Travel light and travel quickly,'* his father had taught him, and it had served him well, getting him out of tricky situations because he was able to move quickly. He would make his way north to one of the cadres he had set up and rebuild the operation. It would be a bigger and much stronger operation; of that he was determined.

'Mike, this is Rick, calling in my official police capacity. Just wanted to let you know that there is now a firearms unit on the plot.'

'Thanks, Rick, I appreciate the heads-up. Let me get my team up to speed and I'll give you the nod in a few minutes.'

'Just one thing, Mike, you mentioned previously about disabling the vehicle. I need whoever is controlling it to be able to revert it back to normal when the firearms unit challenges them. Is that doable?'

'Yes, I'll make sure they're in the vicinity to do that.'

'Update...' said Mike, *'the firearms unit are on the plot, so all units be aware, and with the exception of eight-four and nine-two, move away from the plot. Eight-four, you'll be the firearms team's eyes initially when there is movement in the park. Nine-two, find*

different cover and guide them to the car before they can make their move. I then need you to turn that gadget off so the driver has full control again. I will relay your commentary to them so keep it short, sweet and to the point. Eight-four, did you receive?

'Yes, yes, from eight-four,' Barry replied.

'As soon as they have the men secured, we will pull out, quietly and slowly, with no interaction with anyone else. Is that understood?'

'Yes, yes,' Barry and Lynn acknowledged.

'This is where it gets interesting,' Mike muttered to himself.

'What's the update, Mike?' Trevor asked.

'The firearms unit is on the plot, so you can put the call in, and we can hand it over to them.'

'Excellent, I'll send a message when the call has been placed,' Trevor said, ending the call, before turning to Andy.

'Yep, I got the gist, I'll call our friend now.' Andy picked up the phone. 'I think I'll tease him a little, play the disgruntled partner, that sort of thing.'

Kam answered after just one ring.

'Yes?'

'Mr Kam, you disappoint me. I had heard so many good things about you, and yet you go and spoil everything,' said Andy.

'What are you talking about?' Kam asked, unsure where the conversation was headed. He was angry again to be caught off-guard like this.

'I called and arranged the meeting in good faith so that you can get your money back and we can operate freely in

London without any intrusion from you. Sending your men to the meeting was not a good move, Mr Kam, what were they supposed to do from behind the bushes, attack us? Scare us? What was your objective?'

'I did what anyone else would do, I sent my men to check that you weren't setting a trap,' Kam said, knowing that it would be futile to lie.

'It makes you look a little foolish now, doesn't it? Honestly, if you could see them now, you would shake your head,' Andy said, laughing out loud.

Kam was infuriated but kept his cool, hoping to salvage the situation.

'Why are you calling, to change the meeting?'

'Not at all. I am calling to tell you that the meeting is off. You are not a man with honour, and we can see that we will have to force you out of London the hard way. Expect some resistance from now on, Mr Kam, and we are immensely grateful for the funds you have so graciously provided. The money will go a long way to funding more soldiers to fight you with,' Andy said, laughing again one last time before hanging up.

'You enjoyed that, didn't you?' Trevor asked.

'Yes, I did.'

'My guess is that he'll be calling his men right about now,' Trevor said.

'NINE-TWO,' said Mike, *'are you in position?'*

'Yes, yes, I have good vision on the vehicle,' Lynn replied.

'From the eyeball, all three men now walking towards the main entrance and the vehicle.'

Mike called Rick.

'They're on the move, Rick; I imagine they'll be at the car in about sixty seconds.'

'Thanks, Mike, I'll prep the team. Keep this line open so we can have real-time info.'

'Will do.'

'Now twenty metres from the entrance, I will lose them as soon as they leave the park,' Barry said. *'Now a loss, loss to eight-four, nine-two can you take?'*

'Yes, yes, contact to nine-two. All three men approaching the Jaguar.'

'You hear that, Rick?' Mike asked.

'Yes, the team are aware, there is an open channel. They're in place, don't worry.'

'Standby, doors opening. All three stepping back from the vehicle, I'm guessing from the heat. Now all three into vehicle and doors shut.'

'Rick, over to your guys, mate,' Mike said.

'Already on it, Mike, as you'll soon hear.'

'From nine-two, the vehicle is slowly reversing and inclined to drive towards the south exit. I see brake lights as another vehicle has come into the car park from that same exit, and now another vehicle has driven in from the north exit, boxing the Jaguar in. Standby, I hear lots of shouting, things are about to get very tasty.'

Mike jumped in. *'Nine-two, turn full control back to the driver.'*

'WHAT THE HELL is wrong with the car?' the front passenger asked the driver.

'How the hell do I know? I didn't even know the air conditioning could work when the car was switched off, and none of the window controls are working. Look at all these lights on the dashboard. It's as if the cart is possessed!'

'Can you drive it?'

'Yes, the engine sounds like it's working, although it's making a weird noise. Let's just go, we'll find out soon enough,' the driver said, putting it into reverse and moving slowly out of the parking space.

The driver turned the wheel and edged out, aiming to face south and go back the way they'd come in. As he moved towards the entrance, another car came in, blocking the way out of the narrow exit.

'Bloody fool,' the driver cursed, waving his arms for the other car to move back. The dark blue BMW SUV did not go back but continued to drive towards them, stopping less than a foot from their front bumper.

'What is he doing?' the passenger asked, watching the dark-clothed driver as he stared at them. The three men were so focused on the BMW that they didn't notice a similar car come in from the other exit behind them and stop inches away. It was only when they saw a passenger getting out that they realised something was wrong. The passenger was wearing tactical gear and carrying a weapon that was now pointed directly at the driver.

'Armed police!'

'Quick, reverse!' the passenger said.

'It's too late,' the driver replied, having seen the car blocking them from behind. He raised his hands in the air, showing them to the police officer. The driver of the BMW also got out and raised his weapon, as did the two officers from the vehicle behind.

'Armed police! Driver, open your window slowly with one

hand, keep the other one raised. The rest of you, keep your hands up where we can see them!'

'Damn!' said the rear passenger. He raised one hand in the air whilst surreptitiously calling Kam on his phone with the other, dropping the phone onto the seat when he did so, before raising his other hand quickly.

'Do as they say, I don't want to die in this cursed country,' the driver said calmly, resigned to his fate. Strangely, the lights on the dashboard had stopped flashing and when he pressed the button to open his window, it worked just fine.

'Use your other hand to reach out and open the door, keep the other hand up where I can see it!' the officer shouted.

The driver did as he was told, opening his door.

'Use your knee to open it further, I want to see both hands! Get out of the vehicle and turn around, hands up until I tell you otherwise!'

The driver obliged.

'Now, get on your knees first, and then lie down on your stomach. You can use your hands when you lie down and then put them out to the side!'

The driver braced himself for the contact that was about to happen.

The officer's colleague knelt alongside him, pulling his arms together so that he could handcuff him with zip-ties. He used two for extra security. When the driver's hands were secure, the officer patted him down, quickly removing the handgun that the suspect had tucked in his belt.

'Gun!' the officer shouted, showing it to his colleague before putting it down behind him, out of reach. He continued with his search and removed a mobile phone, cigarettes, a lighter, and a wallet, placing them in a small pile with the gun. When he was satisfied there was nothing else, he stood, picked up the possessions, and placed them in an evidence bag.

'Rear passenger on my side, open your window and then reach out and open your door. I want to see your hands at all times!' another officer shouted.

The process was repeated until all three men had been secured. The Jaguar was then searched, and the rear passenger's phone located. The number it had called was noted and the phone switched off. That information was passed to the team leader, who was sitting in another vehicle nearby as back-up. Rick Watts was then also informed.

Once the car had been searched, the officers were satisfied the threat was over. They watched over the prisoners until a van arrived to take them away for processing, where they would spend several years in prison at His Majesty's pleasure.

'Quang! What is happening?' Kam shouted after receiving the call.

It was then that he heard the police officer ordering his man out of the vehicle. He hung his head in disappointment, before looking up at the ceiling and cursing in his own language.

'Damn them all!' he said out loud.

It was the confirmation he needed: his time in London was up, and he needed to get away.

Now.

'That's all three men now in custody,' Lynn relayed to her team as she watched the arrests play out less than a hundred yards away.

'All units, it's a stand down, stand down, let's regroup for a debrief at the rendezvous point,' Mike said. *'Great job, team, really great job.'*

24

MARYAM

'Rick just called. All three men have been detained by the Specialist Firearms Command unit, all in possession of handguns. Their phones have been seized, but one of them managed to get a call to a number which Rick believes may be Kam's. That leaves just Kam himself in the London area now, so expect movement from him at any time,' Kendra said.

'Great news. And to be honest, we want him to go on the run so he can't put a stop to our evil plan to steal his properties,' Andy said.

'So, what next?' Trevor asked, 'any suggestions?'

'I think we keep teasing him and hope it drives him mad enough to run faster. Want me to give him a call?' Andy asked.

'Just to be clear, we have a tag on his car, and we can track his phone, yes?' Kendra asked.

'That's right, love. The only thing we should worry about is if he dumps them both, then we have no way of tracking him, do we?'

'You'd think that, wouldn't you?' Andy said, 'but there are other ways of tracking him, which I have put into motion.'

'What's that, Andy?' Kendra asked.

'Remember, we hacked into his computers, and that's how we got all the information on the properties and the bank accounts. What that has allowed me to do is upload some sneaky software that tells me when anyone has logged into the company computer accounts, bank accounts, all of them. If he does a runner and tries to log into a computer anywhere, I'll know, wherever he is.'

'That'll help, for sure. Hopefully it will be somewhere we can go and pick him up,' Trevor said.

'On that note, there's something you should know about Kam. Apart from his minions all over the country, he has some serious connections overseas who he may call upon to help him out. That's why we need to take him out of action quickly, before he has a chance of recovering anything of his operation,' Andy said.

'Are you suggesting anything?' Kendra asked.

'I am. I think we need to put so much pressure on him that he has no choice but to leave the country, which is where we can step in and pick him up.' Andy grinned knowingly.

'How?' Trevor asked.

'Another thing you should know about Kam is that he has a boat.'

RAYMOND KAM WAS NOW a man on the run, not just from the authorities but from a mysterious organisation that had likely been the cause of all his recent problems. As hard as he tried, he couldn't think of anyone who could be responsible, which frustrated him on many levels. He was now on his own and his choices were limited. He could call upon his connections up north to come to his aid and to keep him safe until he could rebuild. He could call upon his American cousins to give him sanctuary, but that would leave him thousands of miles away at a time when he may need to be much closer if he was going to rebuild. Or he could stay with his connections in Calais, where he could direct his operations and be close enough to have an impact on the rebuilding. It would cost him a percentage of his business, but it would be worth it, with the added bonus of having a foothold in Europe, where he'd always planned to expand.

His decision made, he was away from the house within minutes with nothing but his backpack and phone. His plan was simple: escape at all costs.

'Yep, I reckon that's where he's going, for sure,' Andy said confidently, as he tracked Kam's vehicle.

'What can we do?' Kendra asked.

'We can't let him get away, that's for sure,' said Trevor.

'At some point, he's going to get rid of the car, and maybe the phone, too, so we need to act fast,' Andy suggested.

'Got any suggestions?' Trevor asked.

'How soon can we get someone to Limehouse?'

'You want us to do what?' Mo asked when Trevor had called.

'We want you to sabotage a boat. It shouldn't be too difficult, surely, for someone with your skills.'

'Where is this boat?' Mo asked.

'It's at the Limehouse Marina, and you need to move fast because our man is going to be there in about half an hour. We're going to try and stall him but do it on the hurry-up.'

'We're on our way. I may leave this one to Amir, he's better at that sort of thing than I am.'

'Be careful, he's probably armed and he's certainly desperate, so he won't be happy if he sees someone on his boat.'

'Understood. Call me if anything changes,' Mo said, 'we're about fifteen minutes away.'

Mo and Amir had been near their mother's home in Ilford when Trevor had called, having sent them and the team home earlier due to the day's developments, so they were well-placed to get to Kam's boat before he did.

Andy had messaged the details of the boat at the marina, which was moored at jetty B. The Beneteau Gran Turismo 46 was a striking fourteen-metre cruiser that could accommodate six people in luxury, with all the modern inventory that Kam had insisted upon. Its twin Volvo engines packed a mighty punch and gave him the performance he'd requested.

None of his men were aware of the boat; it was his personal sanctuary from the world when he wanted to get away from his responsibilities, and where he had frequently brought his mistress, the daughter of a wealthy London-based Qatari sheikh who had been furious when the relationship had been discovered. Kam never saw her again. He missed her deeply and had made a desperate attempt to get her back. This had led to a confrontation with the sheikh and his men, and a fight had ensued, resulting in the only time

Kam had been arrested, for common assault on the sheikh. Although he hadn't been charged, the arrest was on record and the team were now aware of it.

Tragedy soon followed when the sheikh's daughter had taken her life as a result, something that had affected Kam deeply. It was the reason he hadn't visited the boat for some time now, the painful memories a reminder of that tragedy. He had no choice now, though; if he were to leave the country and get to the safety of his colleagues in Calais, the boat was his best hope.

As he drove, his current predicament quickly came back to him and he shook his head in regret. He cleared his head, thinking ahead and trying to formulate his escape with minimal fuss. He was not expecting the call.

'Mr Kam, have you given up already? It's not like you to tuck your tail between your legs and run away so fast, I am surprised,' Andy told him.

'I told you, I will not be doing business in London, so you can stop calling me.'

'Well, I suppose we could, but it wouldn't be much fun, would it? I tell you what, I'll give you a chance, some hope, even. I will tell my men not to hurt you if you can escape the net that is quickly closing around you. If you can evade them and leave London, then you won't hear from me again. But while you are in London, and I see that you still are, then you are game. How's that?'

'How do you...' Kam spluttered. He could hear laughter.

'Ah, Mr Kam, you have so much to learn,' Andy said, before ending the call.

Kam knew he was in deep trouble when he realised he was being tracked. He looked in the rearview mirrors trying to see if anyone was following and knew that he had to abandon the car and his phone as soon as possible if he was going to have a chance of getting to the marina.

He joined the A13 towards central London and continued to look for anyone following. He saw signs for the Beckton retail park and turned off. He parked the Porsche outside Topps Tiles and walked away in a hurry, whilst checking through his phone for the Uber app. He booked a ride that was due in six minutes and put the location for the pickup as outside the Iceland supermarket. He walked towards it and kept looking around for anyone following him, his hackles well and truly up, his demeanour now one of fear. While he waited for the black Toyota Prius to turn up, he kept checking his phone for an ETA. When he finally spotted the cab, he put his arm up to attract the driver's attention and headed towards it. Just before he reached the back, he threw his phone in the bin outside the supermarket, having paid for the cab in advance.

'Mr Chang?' the driver asked when Kam opened the door.

'Yes,' Kam replied, acknowledging his alias.

'Narrow Street, sir?' the driver asked.

'Yes, La Figa Italian restaurant.'

'I'll have you there in fifteen minutes, sir.'

Kam smiled and breathed a sigh of relief. His confidence was coming back now that he knew they couldn't track him anymore.

'IT LOOKS like he's dumped the car and the phone at that retail park.'

'Any news from Mo or Amir?' Trevor asked.

'They've arrived at the marina, but I haven't heard anything else.'

'I'll send a message telling them that Kam has dumped the car and is probably on his way there now,' Kendra said.

'Let's hope you're right, Andy, and he's going to the boat, otherwise we'll have to wait for him to log on somewhere. That could take days, which I'd rather not give him,' Trevor said.

'I don't think he has any choice, Trevor; the boat is his best chance of getting out of the country, knowing that he's got police and a mystery man after him. Where else could he go in London?'

'I suppose we'll find out very soon, won't we?' said Trevor.

THE MARINA WASN'T FENCED off and security was limited to metal gates at the jetties, allowing Mo and Amir to walk freely around, figuring the place out as they did so. Bizarrely, although the gate was a robust one, there was no real fencing on either side of it, just some ornate posts and chains that were more symbolic than a deterrent. Someone could easily step over.

'That is weird, bro, all that effort into a gate but almost unimpeded access to the jetties everywhere else?' Amir said.

'I'm not complaining, it makes it easy for us, doesn't it? There's jetty B over there, let's find a place to climb over,' Mo said.

There were a few pedestrians walking around and some of them nonchalantly stepped over the chains and took a natural shortcut to the jetty of their choice. It seemed to be the norm, and nobody challenged them.

'Here we go,' Amir said, doing the same and stepping over towards the concrete jetty.

They walked along, looking for the boat Andy had told them about.

'What's the name of it again?' Amir asked.

'Maryam,' Mo replied.

'That was his girlfriend's name, wasn't it?'

'Yes.'

'There she is,' Amir said, nodding towards the sleek white cruiser with its black detailing, moored tightly to the jetty, the name *Maryam* proudly emblazoned in elegantly formed gold letters on its stern.

Mo could see that it was simple enough to get on board and assumed that the cockpit would be locked, which they needed to access. Glancing around to see if anyone was watching, they stepped onto the boat as if they belonged and walked calmly towards the cockpit's fully glazed patio doors, which were, indeed, locked.

'Do your thing, maestro,' Mo said to his brother.

Amir leaned forward and used his pick lock to gain entry, taking less than ten seconds.

'After you, your highness.' he said, bowing to his elder brother.

They walked in and locked the doors behind them. Andy had given them full specs of the boat and they knew where to aim for. The engines were accessed by a large centre hatch that encompassed the saloon and aft deck, and they quickly opened it and took the steps down. The twin Volvo engines looked imperious, and Amir shook his head sadly.

'What is it?'

'Such a shame to do this,' Amir said, 'they are a thing of beauty.'

He took out a multi-tool and opened it up, revealing the scissors. He reached down and cut two wires that were hidden from view and pulled their corresponding connectors, which led to sensors. He then pulled two additional connectors out from the engines themselves; something that would be more visible, were Kam to check.

'Will that stop it from running?' Mo asked.

'Yes, without good electrics, none of these modern boats can function properly, so this lovely thing will not be moving an inch.'

'Okay, that's our job done, then, let's go,' Mo said, standing in readiness.

'Bro, we may have disabled the boat, but we still have to grab the bastard, don't we?'

'Yeah, but Trevor didn't ask us to do that bit, did he?'

'He didn't have to, bro. Who else is going to do it? Think about it.' Amir took out one of the Tasers that he'd brought along, and a couple of zip-ties.

Mo took a few seconds, trying to come up with ways to avoid a confrontation with an armed man.

'Come on, bro, haven't we been shot enough times?' he pleaded, 'and anyway, how are we gonna get the bastard out of here?'

'That part is easy,' Mo said, 'we'll just use his boat.'

'The one you just disabled?' Mo asked, his arms up in the air in exasperation.

Amir laughed.

'Bro, it's two wires, which I can reconnect. Relax, will you?'

25

CAPTURE

Kam waited for the Prius to drive off. Happy that the cab was out of view, he crossed over to Narrow Street before turning left into Horseferry Road. Although more confident, he still took the time to look around, and when he was sure he wasn't being followed, he turned off again and walked into Goodhart Place, a shortcut to the marina. The small housing estate offered good cover and the alleyway at the river end brought him out close to the jetty gate.

As with most others, he elected to step over the low fencing and walk towards the jetty. After one last look, he walked onto jetty B towards where the *Maryam* was berthed. As he approached the boat his memories came back, the hairs on his neck standing up. He shook his head, sadness overwhelming him. He had paid for the regular maintenance and cleaning of the boat, so he would be ready to leave as soon as the boat was warmed up and ready. He took a minute to remove the two mooring lines in preparation for leaving, before unlocking the cockpit doors and stepping inside, closing the doors behind him.

Breathing a sigh of relief, he took off his jacket and walked straight towards the helm. He placed the backpack on the double-seat bench next to the captain's chair and turned on the battery switches that were to the side of his position. He then opened the small fridge on the other side of the boat and took out a lanyard and key that were hidden in an empty ice cube container. This he placed in the dashboard to allow for the engines to start up. Making sure the motors were in neutral, he turned the key to start the engines, waiting for the low rumble he had been so fond of.

There was no rumble or noise of any kind. He removed the key and reinserted it, before attempting again. Nothing happened.

'What the hell is wrong now?' he shouted.

Taking a deep breath, he tried a third time to no avail, so he sat back to think. Knowing that the boat was regularly serviced, he swore at the mechanic he had entrusted to keep the boat running and in good shape. He walked back to the engine hatch that was in the middle of the deck and opened it. Taking the steps down carefully, he examined the pristine engines to see if anything looked out of place, and noticed the two connectors had come loose. Shaking his head, he put them back, before going back up to try again, wondering how they had come loose.

The fourth attempt was the same as the first three: nothing at all happened. There was nothing to indicate anything was wrong, no warning lights, no lights of any kind. He swore again. Kam took a bottle of water from the small fridge and took a large swig. He wasn't sure what he would do next. He daren't contact anyone in case he was tracked again.

It had been a difficult, tiring day, so he decided to take some time to rest and try again later. Before going to his cabin, he went down into the galley to check on supplies for his journey, nodding in appreciation that the fridge there was stocked with water and other drinks.

He checked the cupboard stores and found them full of basics such as tea, coffee, sugar, biscuits, and some tinned food he had stocked the last time he was here. He had no intention of doing a last-minute shop, so he was happy to see that it wouldn't be necessary. The supplies were more than enough to get him to Calais. He went back up to the deck and down the small steps into the spacious main cabin, which evoked many fond memories.

He saw the stranger and the yellow gun-shaped weapon pointing straight at him but had no time to respond before he felt the pain searing through his body. He fell forward, narrowly missing the intruder, who stepped to one side and continued to press the trigger on the Taser. The pain was intense. The only consolation was that he landed on the plush bed that he had been so looking forward to sleeping in again. He said just one word before he passed out.

'*Maryam.*'

'H*I*, Mo. Is the boat out of action? Need to know so that we can plan the next steps,' Kendra asked when she called.

'Erm, no, Amir decided to fix it instead.'

'Huh?'

'We decided to take the initiative and change the plan a touch,' Mo said. 'I hope that doesn't cause any problems.'

'It does, Mo. We're in the process of sending Rick's team

to go and apprehend Kam. Where the hell is he? Didn't he turn up? You just decided to steal his boat?'

'Erm, it's not entirely like that. You can cancel sending anyone for Kam, he's having a nap in his bunk, but he won't be going anywhere except for Tilbury. I hope that's okay?'

'Mo, you've lost me, will you please tell me what the hell is going on? Where's Amir?'

'He's just opening the lock so we can leave the marina.'

'What? What the hell is happening?'

'Kam is taking a nap and we're bringing him to the factory... in his boat,' Mo said.

'You've taken Kam prisoner and stolen his boat and now you're coming to us,' she said, 'did I get that right?'

'Yes, you did. I figure we'll be at our jetty in a couple of hours. Can someone meet us there so we can transport him to the factory?'

'Hang on, my dad wants to speak with you,' she said, and handed the phone to Trevor.

'Uh-oh,' Mo replied.

'*Uh-oh,* is that all you can say? Are you two nuts? We told you he's a lunatic with a gun and you decide to take him on?'

'To be fair, he didn't really have a chance to pull his gun, Trevor; Amir tasered him good and proper,' Mo replied.

'It was his idea, wasn't it?'

'Well... yes, no point in denying it,' Mo said, 'but it makes sense, Trevor. If the police take him into custody, he'll probably get off with a light sentence or nothing at all. This way, we can decide what to do with him, can't we?'

'Just get back as soon as you can. How the hell do you know how to drive the boat, anyway?' Trevor asked.

'Not me, I haven't got a clue. It's my brother, he's been going out with Andy on *Soggy Bottom* and has learned a few things,' Mo replied, referring to the team boat that had been gifted by a grateful hacker Andy had helped earn a fortune.

'Has he, though?' Trevor asked, 'I mean, they are two very different boats, aren't they?'

'He seems confident, what can I say. He's back, so we'd better get going. See you in a couple of hours,' Mo said, abruptly ending the call. He could sense Trevor shaking his head in disapproval and grinned as Amir came back to the helm to guide the boat out of the lock.

'What are you grinning at?' Amir asked.

'Not a lot. Just told the team what we're doing, and it was met with disapproval.'

Amir laughed.

'Damn, I wish I'd heard that. Anyway, I just need to get through this lock and go back and close it, so give me a minute.' Amir moved the throttle forward gently to take *Maryam* out of the lock. 'Back in a minute, bro,' he added.

Mo watched his younger sibling run back to the lock and close the gate, before walking back to the boat.

'Damn, that brother of mine can do just about anything,' he muttered proudly.

They were soon under way, eastbound along the river Thames, aiming for the jetty where *Soggy Bottom* was berthed.

Where the fate of Kam and the gang members still held at the factory was to be decided.

THEY WERE MET at the jetty by Darren, Izzy and Jimmy, who helped the now-awake Kam to his feet and out of the boat. It was a short walk to the factory where they searched him thoroughly before securing him in one of the empty rooms.

'This was all he brought with him,' Mo told the team when they had adjourned for a debriefing. 'A backpack filled with money, spare ammo, a couple of passports, phones, and a laptop.'

'Oh, goody, more to add to the booty we've taken from him,' Andy said, reaching for the laptop that he hoped would reveal more contacts to add to their growing database of bad guys.

'What are we going to do with the prisoners, Trevor?' Darren asked.

'You've got the container ready, so one option is to send the gangsters somewhere far, far away. Not sure about Kam, we're going to do some searching for anyone that might want to have a quiet word in his ear, maybe the FBI or Interpol, or farther afield. Andy will do his thing and find out,' Trevor replied.

'Whatever we decide, it would be good to have them out of here as soon as possible,' Kendra said, 'I'm not keen on keeping them even another day.'

'I'll call our old friend Bruno down at the docks, he may know people who can take the prisoners off our hands and put them to good use for a change,' Trevor said.

'I'll go and start checking to see whoever is a fan of Kam,' Andy said, walking off with the laptop.

'Guys and girls, great work, all of you. It's been a tricky one, but we've taken some really nasty people off the streets of London and put a horrible organisation out of business. There's still plenty to do, but for now, get yourselves some rest and we'll regroup tomorrow with some decisions,' Trevor told the gathering.

There were a couple of tired *whoops* and some high-fives as the team made their way out, leaving Kendra and Trevor alone.

'I'll give Rick a call, Dad, and let him know we're almost done. Anything else need doing?'

'Not today, love, let's get some rest. I'm sure we'll come up with something after we've had some sleep.'

'Okay, I'll catch you up, let me go and say goodnight to Andy,' she said, kissing her father on the cheek.

Trevor smiled as he watched her walk away.

Don't mess this up, Andy, he thought.

ANDY WAS LINKING the laptop to one of the monitors and looked up as Kendra walked in, surprised to see her.

'I shouldn't be too long, Kendra, let me just have a quick check on this laptop and I'll leave,' he said.

'Okay, I'll wait with you,' she said, smiling as she sat down.

Andy was about to tell her not to bother, before he realised that she was waiting on him to continue their discussion. He steadied himself and paused before speaking.

'We should go on a date,' he said suddenly.

The shock on her face spoke volumes.

'W-what?'

'You heard me, we should go on a date.'

'Andy, we've been through this, we made a deal, remember?'

'I know, I know, but someone reminded me that things were very different back then. We're a much bigger, more experienced and competent team, with lots of modern technology, it's miles away from when we made our deal. I don't want to take a chance that anything happens to one of us, because we'll both regret it if we don't give us a go,' he said.

'What's brought this on, all of a sudden?'

'Actually, it was your dad. He told me that we'd both regret it, and he reminded me that things are nothing like they were. He's right, too, and he didn't threaten me or anything!'

'My dad? Are you serious?'

'I know, I was just as shocked as you are!' Andy stood and approached Kendra, taking her hands in his.

'I think he's absolutely right. I don't want to think about anything bad happening to either of us, I want to think about something good happening *with* us,' he said softly, reaching in and kissing her gently on the lips.

She didn't resist.

EPILOGUE

Central Africa

The container that the team had prepped for the eight gang members arrived on time and was met by the contingent that Bruno had arranged two weeks earlier. Bruno had connections throughout the world's ports, especially the more obscure or remote ones where bribes were made to conceal cargo, and in this case, an entire container. After being dropped off in a remote desert location, it was opened.

The men who opened it were about to be hit by an overwhelming stench; a stench that came from a dozen men being enclosed in a metal box for two weeks. After opening the doors, they quickly stepped back. They waited patiently for the prisoners to make their way out slowly, covering their eyes from the intense daylight. Eventually, they were all out in the open and were provided with a bottle of water each.

A tall, uniformed man, holding a small cane, stepped forward to greet them.

'Welcome, legionnaires,' he said, addressing them all, 'I am Staff Sergeant Lamare. You will address me as Staff Sergeant Lamare at all times. Do you understand?'

There was a pause before one of the braver prisoners stepped forward.

'Where the hell are we? Who are you lot?' he asked, his south London accent masked slightly by the croak in his voice.

The cane was vicious as it struck him on the back of the leg.

'You will listen or you will feel pain, it is very simple. I told you once and I will not tell you again, you will address me as Sergeant Lamare. Do you understand me?'

The man he had struck, now on one knee, put an arm out in supplication.

'Y... yes, Staff Sergeant Lamare,' he said quickly.

'That's good. Do the rest of you understand?' the sergeant shouted, looking at them each in turn.

'Yes, Staff Sergeant Lamare,' they said weakly.

'Good, good, this looks like it will be a good set of new recruits, unlike the last delivery,' Lamare said, nodding appreciatively. 'We always welcome new blood here.'

'Sergeant... Staff Sergeant Lamare, please, where are we?' the man asked respectfully.

'You are in the most inhospitable desert that any military force is operating, soldier. We are hundreds of miles from civilisation.'

'S... soldier, Staff Sergeant Lamare?'

'Yes, soldier, you are all now proud members of the French Foreign Legion,' Lamare said, 'and that over there will be your home for the next twenty years,' he added, pointing his cane to a dull, sand-coloured fort in the near distance.

'Tw-twenty years? Twenty years?' the man asked, before adding 'Staff Sergeant Lamare?'

'Twenty years, soldier. Now get up, you'll be put to work immediately. You will pay for all the crimes you have committed, all of you.'

Two of the gang members passed out and most of the rest cried softly in resignation, knowing that anything more would lead to a swipe from the cane.

New York

Raymond Kam woke suddenly when he was slammed against the rear seats of the van that was transporting him on the final leg of what had been a lengthy journey. It had taken a week for the ship to reach the east coast, arriving at the port of Boston, where Bruno had arranged for him to be taken on a four-hour journey to New York City. The ride in the back had been excruciatingly uncomfortable, so he was relieved when the van came to a sudden stop, despite his side aching from the impact.

The doors were opened, and Kam was pulled out roughly by his feet and thrown to the floor. When his eyes acclimatised, he raised his head to see four men looking down at him. One of them took a deep drag from his cigarette before putting it out on the floor. He exhaled the smoke towards Kam before speaking in Vietnamese.

'Welcome home, Raymond,' the smoker said, grinning at the surprised look on Kam's face.

'Where am I?'

The four men laughed.

'You're back where you belong, Raymond; New York City.

I have to say, what a great surprise and pleasure it was to find out that you were being sent to us,' the man said.

'And just who the hell are you?' Kam demanded.

The largest of the men stepped forward and punched Kam viciously in the stomach, forcing him to drop to one knee.

'We *were* destined to be the greatest Vietnamese gang in history before your father and his cronies left us to form the abomination you called *Born to Kill*,' the man said, stepping towards Kam and leaning down to stare into his eyes. 'It's taken us many, many years, but we are still here, still successful and still together.'

Kam spluttered, struggling to breathe.

'I have no clue who you are and what you are talking about,' he replied, 'I was just a kid.'

'The sins of the father, blah, blah,' the man continued, 'well, you know what they say. We haven't forgotten, and it is time for you to pay back some of that dishonour.'

'What the hell are you talking about? Who are you?'

The four men laughed again.

'We're the *Vietnamese Flying Dragons*, Mr Kam, and you will be punished for the sins of your father and the others who abandoned us as they did.'

The Factory, **Tilbury**

'So, to summarise, we ended up with a bunch of prisoners that we'd rather not have had, and we've decided what we'll be doing with them,' Sir Robert told Trevor as they sat in the canteen for coffee.

'I'm guessing it's because of the secret nature of the operation, right?' Trevor grinned.

'You would be correct. To be honest, nobody is going to miss the Vietnamese gangsters, are they? And Reg Malone and his two accomplices can pay for their sins by doing some hard labour alongside them when they arrive,' Sir Robert continued.

'Arrive where, exactly?'

The admiral laughed before answering.

'Honestly, I think it was a genius move, if I may say so myself. We're sending them to what is probably the most remote place on earth, a thousand miles from the nearest land, which happens to be Africa.'

'Please don't keep me in suspense,' Trevor laughed.

'We're sending them to Ascension Island in the South Atlantic,' the admiral replied.

'That tiny island we have an airbase on?'

'That's the one. At the moment, it's a holding facility for a bunch of illegal migrants who were on their way to America from Sri Lanka and ended up there instead. Our guests can be put to work helping them out and doing some general maintenance duties on the base.'

'Isn't anyone likely to say anything?' Trevor asked.

'Well, we've been a little sneaky and given them all new identities and signed them up as local workers, so even if someone mentions it, we have paperwork in place that suggests it's all by the book. That was after they were given the choice: pay for their sins or disappear forever, which they took seriously. We'll keep them there for a few years before we decide what we're going to do. Until then, they will work for their food and lodgings,' the admiral said.

'I think it's a great idea. It's all ended up as it should, the weapons retrieved, the bad guys out of action for many, many years, and a satisfied customer. I hope you give us a good review, Admiral,' Trevor joked.

Sir Robert laughed.

'A review is the least of what you'll be receiving, old chap. I have a list of jobs that I think your team would be eminently suitable for; are you up for it?'

'Does it pay well?'

'Yes, I believe it does,' the admiral said.

'Then let's get to it,' Trevor said, reaching out and shaking hands with the First Sea Lord.

AZURE HOTEL, **London Docklands**

'I'm actually stunned that we managed to get away with this,' Andy said, 'without getting beaten half to death by your dad, anyway.'

'It's just for a few days, silly, nobody will miss us,' Kendra said, cuddling up closer.

'When are they starting work to rebuild it?' Andy asked, stroking her hair. 'I mean, most of the rooms are like this, in really good shape and not needing a lot. It's just the ground and first couple of floors, isn't it?'

'Yes, and they start the day after tomorrow. We have enough supplies to enjoy tomorrow also, so stop worrying about it and pass me another glass of champagne.'

'Mr Khan is a good man for letting us stay,' Andy said, passing her the glass.

'To be honest, apart from the unfortunate death of his son, he's done quite well out of it, hasn't he? He got rid of the threat, he got rid of the debt, and he can start again fresh.'

'He's in for a shock in a few weeks.' Andy laughed.

'Why?'

'One of the hotels we stole from Kam was actually bought legitimately, there were no threats made or debt to pay off or anything like that. They were making so much money they actually bought it for cash. And we're going to give it to Mr Khan so he and his family can run it. Hopefully that will make up for some of his loss.'

'That's a great gesture, Andy. What about the rest?'

'Most of them will be going back to the victims, we're doing it through a legitimate law firm and anonymously to limit the attention it gets. Some of the money we grabbed will go towards those who need it because of Kam's organisation. The majority of it will help us grow further.'

'Yeah, Dad told me that Mike Romain accepted his offer to merge with us. It cost a bit but, damn, it's worth every penny,' Kendra said.

'Yep, and as we grow, we'll get busier, so having breaks like this is going to be harder, you know that, right?'

'I know, but at least we're not waiting until we're old and grey before giving us a shot, plus what we do is also very satisfying and a lot of fun,' she replied.

'And dangerous!' He laughed.

'Yes, there is that, but it's worth it, right?'

'Absolutely,' he replied, leaning over and kissing her again.

THE END

ACKNOWLEDGMENTS

As ever, my thanks go to you for your ongoing support with this series. I will endeavour to keep you entertained for years to come.

I'd also like to thank Vince Elflain, John Ludwig and Richard Fidge for their assistance, guidance, and support with some of the police-related information (none of it confidential, I should add). I'm a stickler for getting it right, and their assistance has been invaluable.

Linda Nagle has done her usual fabulous work as editor and I must also give huge thanks go to my partner, Alison, for her help with the cover for this book and for her ongoing support, without which I'd have written a lot less books.

Again, my thanks to you all.
TH

ABOUT THE AUTHOR

Theo Harris is an emerging author of crime action novels. He was born in London, raised in London, and became a cop in London.

Having served as a police officer in the Metropolitan Police service for thirty years, he witnessed and experienced the underbelly of a capital city that you are never supposed to see.

Theo was a specialist officer for twenty-seven of the thirty years and went on to work in departments that dealt with serious crimes of all types. His experience, knowledge and connections within the organisation have helped him with his storytelling, with a style of writing that readers can associate with.

Theo has many stories to tell, starting with the 'Summary Justice' series featuring DC Kendra March, and will follow with many more innovative, interesting, and fast-paced stories for many years to come.

For more information about upcoming books please visit theoharris.co.uk

Printed in Great Britain
by Amazon